IN PLAIN SIGHT

IN PLAIN SIGHT

Wolves of Collier Pack

By

Julie Trettel

In Plain Sight
Wolves of Collier Pack: Book Three
Copyright ©2019, Julie Trettel. All rights reserved.
Cover Art by, Bridgette O'Hare of Dark Unicorn Designs
Editing by, Sara Meadows of TripleA Publishing Services

Thanks and Acknowledgments

A huge thanks to my friends, family, and editing/cover staff. I was ready to give up and push this book back. I hate missing deadlines, but after some bad health everything fell behind. You guys really rallied behind me and gave me the encouragement and support necessary to not only finish this book, but to finish it on time! WE DID IT!!!

Bran

Chapter 1

"Branimir, my beloved, rise."

I slowly stood, legs trembling from kneeling for too long. "I pledge my allegiance to you, Alpha," I said formally, careful to keep my eyes downcast in sovereign respect.

"I know the anger and hatred that runs deep within you. Channel that as you move forward on this most sacred mission. The Westins killed your father, your birth Alpha, and they continue to harbor the demon, Elena. Your journey will not be an easy one, but if you vow under the sacred blood oath to avenge your father, you will forever live in reverence and gratitude in this world and into the next by all true Bulgarian wolves. Do you so accept?"

I didn't look around. Not a single breath could be heard as they waited for my response.

"I do. I swear to enact the wishes of my Alpha, or die trying."

I looked up to face my Alpha. He smiled down at me, and I shuddered in his presence. Taking out a small dagger, he held it up for all to see, then passed it to me. The blade stung as it cut through my calloused hand.

I returned the dagger to him and he surprised me as he twisted off the top of the blade. I watched as my blood dripped into the hidden amulet in the dagger's hilt. Securing the top, he handed it to the Pack Witch. I found it mildly ironic that he insisted on keeping a witch when he was so hellbent on killing the lost triplet, Elena—or

Kelsey Westin, as she now was called—for being a witch. I knew there was more to it than that, but the irony was not lost on me.

The witch said some words and I watched the amulet glow. "It is done. From this moment forward you are bound by blood to obey the wishes of your Alpha," she said at last, passing the dagger back to my Alpha. He looked it over, and, satisfied, handed it back to me.

"Sir?"

"I know you will take good care of it, my beloved. It will guide you to my wishes. Bon voyage and safe travels."

"I will not let you down," I vowed.

The Alpha turned and left as the murmurs began throughout the room. It was done. I would be on the next flight to America, and the most important mission of my life was about to begin.

Nothing could get in my way.

Ruby

Chapter 2

I was awake before my alarm clock sounded. I didn't know why I even bothered with the thing. I woke to the sun just as the animals around the farm did each morning. I turned on the radio as I headed into the bathroom, then sang along as I showered and threw my unruly, curly, red, mass of hair into a messy bun. I dressed in worn jeans and a thick flannel shirt.

Signs of spring were all around, but the early mornings were still crisp with the chill of the final days of winter. I tugged on my favorite work boots, turned off the radio, and headed to my kitchen, still humming the last song played.

I had my routine down tight. A pancake topped with one fried egg and two slices of bacon, the precooked kind I just heated up in the microwave simply to save time. Orange juice rounded out my breakfast. I loved coffee, just not first thing in the morning. The pot was on a timer and already filling the house with the delicious aroma.

I ate, poured the entirety of the coffee into a thermos, and headed out the door, down the stairs and right into the barn. It had taken some convincing for my father to agree to let one of his daughters literally live in a barn, even while teasing that my mother had always chased behind me screaming, "Shut the door, Ruby. You don't live in a barn!" Well, now I did, and I loved it.

For the most part my life was very simple. I was the only one of us seven kids to really take to the animals. Well, I guess you could say Clara did, too. She had gone on to university to become a veterinarian and I knew she loved caring for the animals, just not in the same manner as I did.

I had chosen not to go to college, which was a huge disappointment to our parents after both my older two sisters had gone on to excel in advanced degrees. I was just a wild child no one expected to ever amount to much. "Spoiled, "pampered," and "overly dramatic" were common descriptions attached to Ruby Collier. I was okay with it.

I was the middle daughter, after all. Mom says I was born running, always trying to keep up with my older sisters. I grew up with skinned knees and the occasional black eyes, a complete tomboy helping out around the farm. I loved my life and wouldn't trade it for anything. It had made me tough and opinionated. I certainly wasn't afraid to speak out. Sometimes I was accused of just trying to shock people with my words, but honestly, that wasn't it. I just said what I thought and to hell with anyone's feelings.

All my life I had wanted to be nothing more than a cowgirl. Now, here I was living my dream. Maybe others didn't understand it, but for me, life was pretty damn near perfect.

On rare occasions, I envied my sisters a little. Three of them had gone on to find their true mates. However, my nights rarely got lonely. There were plenty of eligible men in Collier, and even of the human variety in the next town over. I was never lacking companionship when I wanted it, but I would never settle down for anyone less than my one true mate. Since I was at peace in Collier with no desire to travel, the odds of me ever meeting him were slim.

Looking around the barn, I smiled. I could never just leave my animals and most males expected a girl to follow him to his pack. That wasn't in the cards for me, and I'd choose my life alone any day, anyway. Nothing would convince me to give up this place, not even him.

I set to work feeding the cows in the dairy below my apartment. I loved the smells and sounds of the barns. My Alpha, Thomas, who was also my little brother, wanted to modernize things around here. Make stuff more efficient. I knew he was looking into some automated feeding system, but I had managed to thwart that idea every time he pitched it.

We'd been farming these lands for hundreds of years, and while we had always had animals, the ones for profit were a relatively new addition after a bad crop nearly bankrupted the entire pack.

Still, there wasn't much to caring for the animals. Sure, it was hard work, but I didn't mind, and neither did the cowboys. It gave us a purpose in life to be proud of. I didn't want to just hit a button or go through a checklist to ensure the machines were functioning properly. I loved the hands-on care. Every creature in my charge had a name. I talked to them as I went about my day, and I petted and loved on them, too. Machines couldn't do that for ya.

All that said, I didn't much mind the milking machines for the dairy cattle that Thomas had installed, even before he took over as Alpha. Those made sense. We had too many heads to manually milk them all and keep them happy. But feeding didn't take long. I sighed, knowing it was likely a losing battle. I would slowly be replaced by machines. Cowgirls were a dying breed due to technology, but I'd keep my head up and fight the transition every step of the way.

"Good morning, Mellie," I said as I entered the nursery and saw our latest new mama looking restless. I walked over and petted her. I had never seen a cow with a stomach so big. Davidson said she was having twins, but I was beginning to wonder if there weren't more in there. I lovingly stroked her back. "It won't be much longer, sweet girl."

The nursery was on the backside of the dairy barn. Inside the barn were rows and rows of stalls for the lactating cows to hook up to the milking machine. Some farms just left them attached all the time. That was cruel and unnecessary to me. My girls hooked up in the mornings, then set out to free-range the grounds until mid-afternoon and again in the evenings. Many would argue it was more work than necessary, but my girls were happy and gave me no trouble. I didn't mind the extra work to give them a good life.

The pregnant cows there came in as they got close to delivery and stayed until the young cows were six weeks old. I manually milked them three times a day to increase their production and get them used to the schedule.

After that they moved back into general population with the other mothers. The babies were moved with them to free-range, and then nursed throughout the day until they weaned at around six months, another reason I was so adamant about not leaving them hooked up to machines all day long. Many operations bottle-fed their young to maximize the amount of milk production from the cows. The care of the animals was my number one priority; profit came second to that. Fortunately, while Thomas and I butted heads on many things, he had never argued that point with me.

We were wolf shifters. Carrying an animal spirit within us gave a different outlook and approach to the animals. Sure, many of our practices weren't conventional. Some would even argue our methods were archaic. Every few years we faced an audit by the government. It was a pain in the ass, but necessary to the sustainability of the industry side of farming. While they'd given pointers on how to increase production and streamline our processes, they couldn't argue with my methods or deem anything illegal.

My morning chores completed in relative peace, I decided to take a ride.

"Morning, sweet Ruby," Austin yelled, and waved from the field as I walked over to the horse stables. He was a handsome fella, but too young for me. He was friends with my baby brother, for crying out loud. Not that it would ever stop me from hooking up with a couple of the other Six Pack. For some reason, Austin always just seemed like the youngest of the group. I refused to see him in any other way, though that certainly never stopped him from trying. Truth be told, I liked him trying, which was probably why I'd never hook up with him.

"Ruby Red, is that you?" Mr. Draper hollered out from the stables. He'd been tending to our horses since before I was born.

"Morning, Mr. Draper," I yelled back.

"Ruby, Cochise didn't come back last night. You know that's not like him. Austin and Conlin are about to head on out and look around for him, but if you're planning to go for a ride, do me a favor and keep an eye out, too."

"I will. Thanks for the heads up," I told him.

It wasn't like the old stallion not to come searching for a meal at night. I truly hoped he was okay.

"Want me to saddle Cinnamon up for you?" Mr. Draper offered.

"That would be great, thanks," I said. Normally I would insist on doing it myself, but my brain was already busy calculating out all the places Cochise could have wandered off to.

Conlin led his horse from the barn. The guy was a total stud and we'd been flirting with each other for weeks. "You riding out with us, Ruby?" he asked with a wink and a smile.

"Nah, go on. I'll keep my eye out for him, though, and radio in if I find him."

Conlin nodded and rode out to meet up with Austin. I wasn't far behind them.

"Good morning, Cinnamon. How's my sweet boy?" I cooed at the only true man in my life. Cinnamon and I had grown up together. He was the first horse I'd ever helped bring into this world and I knew from that day on that caring for animals was all I ever wanted to do. He was my best friend and confidant. I loved that horse more than anything.

I mounted him and gave him some more love and encouragement before we headed out at a trot. Mr. Draper opened the gate to the field, and we took off at a full run. Loose strands of hair flew from my bun in wild flames of red. Riding like that with the wind in my hair was as great and as exhilarating as running in my wolf form. It felt just as natural, man and beast as one.

I rode for hours but saw no signs of Cochise. Just as I was about to turn around and head back to the stables, I got a whiff of something foreign in the air. It didn't set my wolf on edge, though— quite the opposite.

I sniffed the air around me in a sort of drug-induced daze. It was the most alluring scent I'd ever encountered, yet there was an edge of danger to it, too. Nervous excitement shook my body. I had to know what that smell was.

I kept Cinnamon at a trot, then slowed to a walk as the scent grew stronger. I narrowed in on a small patch of trees and dismounted to continue tracking on foot. I tied my horse's reigns to a low branch and hesitantly entered the thicket.

Wolf! I caught the distinct aroma of another wolf shifter in the area, but it wasn't Collier, and I was certain it wasn't a Larken wolf, either. Larkens were another local pack. We often had run-ins

13

with them, and had trouble keeping them off Collier land. We had once all been one pack, so their scent was very similar to that of a Collier wolf, but this was definitely not that.

I tiptoed deeper in, one tree at a time, trying not to make a sound. My hands shook, but I wasn't afraid. There was something comforting about the scent. I knew I was downwind and that if I could stay quiet enough, I should be able to sneak up and get a reading on the threat without him or her noticing me. That was my plan, at least.

I picked up a flash of sulfur in the air, then it was gone, followed by cursing from a deep male voice that reverberated through my entire body. I had to squeeze my legs together as my sex clenched at the sound.

I ducked as the man came into view. My voice caught in my throat at the sight and I was paralyzed. I couldn't have moved if I wanted to.

He was wearing tight, lowcut jeans and a white T-shirt that looked like it was molded to his body. My mouth watered. I couldn't see his face, but from his backside he had the most perfect body I'd ever seen.

He was bent over a small stack of kindling, trying to start a fire but struggling. He struck another match as a flash of sulfur hit my nose again and then I watched it die out before it caught. He cursed again, and a flutter ran through my chest at the sound of his voice. In his frustration, his unique scent burst from him, coating the air around me.

I fought back a moan, feeling that headiness I experienced the first time I smelled him.

Mate, my wolf said inside my head.

I froze. *What? That can't be right.*

Mate, the voice insisted again.

My pulse sped up and I struggled to catch my breath as I tried to process what my wolf was telling me. I sat down hard from where I'd been perched in a squat observing him. A stick broke beneath me and I saw his muscles bunch across his shoulders as he changed into predator mode, trying to identify the noise.

I should have moved away. I should have tried to hide myself better, but I was in shock and just stared until his eyes finally found mine and recognition flared in them.

14

This trespasser was my one true mate.

Bran

Chapter 3

At the sound of a twig snapping much too close, my shoulders tensed, and I called my wolf forward to utilize his heightened senses. Someone was here. I could feel it. I cursed myself for being so stupid. I was supposed to be undercover. I needed to be found, but not yet.

I had just arrived in Collier territory. I thought I'd have a few days to get the lay of the land and decide how best to proceed. I was starving, not having eaten in the last twenty-four hours. I had caught a small rabbit while in wolf form but hated eating raw meat. I had been concentrating so hard on starting a stupid fire that I let my guard down, and someone had gotten the drop on me.

My eyes scanned the woods slowly as I turned in a circle, looking for anything suspicious. It could be nothing more than an animal, but I couldn't just take that chance on an assumption. I had been trained better than that.

Nothing looked out of the ordinary as I kept low, continuing my hunt for the source of the sound. Directly behind where I'd been, I met the bluest pair of eyes I'd ever seen. They did not belong to an animal.

I sniffed the air around me, catching only a hint of scent. Female. The girl wasn't moving. She looked shocked, but not frightened. Then it dawned on me: all my wolf's aggression was gone, replaced with a warmth I'd never felt before. I continued to stare deep into her eyes.

Mate.

I shook my head, trying to break the spell she held over me.

Po dyavolite! I swore to myself. This could not be happening. Not now.

I sucked in a deep breath just as the wind shifted and I was assaulted by her full scent. My wolf whimpered in my head, pushing forward to take control and claim our mate.

Po dyavolite! This was really happening.

"Mate, show yourself," I said, finding my voice at last.

The shocked wide eyes turned to indignation as she slowly rose. A mess of fiery red curls topped her head. I slowly devoured her with my eyes, taking in her oversized breasts and small waist. Even in her jeans I could tell she had a tight ass and muscular legs. I had never seen such an enticing creature in my entire life.

Her hands went to her hips as she popped one to the side. I knew instantly this wild beast would be tough to tame. She screamed of trouble. I didn't need this right now with my mission at stake, yet suddenly everything had changed.

My mind considered the options while I fought to keep my hormones from clouding my judgment. I never dreamed in a million years I would find my one true mate, yet here in the middle of nowhere on a potential suicide mission, she had appeared out of thin air. I shook my head and ran my hand over my week-old beard.

"Who are you?" she asked.

Her melodic voice shot straight to my groin. A primal desire took over me. I had to struggle to remember to keep in character with the American accent I had worked hard to perfect.

"My name is Bran. What is yours, mate?" I asked.

"Ruby," she said softly, still looking like she was in some sort of trance.

I didn't sense fear in her and she shook her head like she was fighting to clear it. I suspected she was in shock. Truth be told, I probably was too.

"What are you doing here?" she finally asked.

I cringed, overcome with guilt. This was my mate, but my need for survival overcame that as I grinned and lied to her face.

"I was just passing through. Heard that maybe Collier Pack would take on a drifter like me for the season. You are the last thing I expected to find," I confessed. That part was at least true enough. "Come here," I told her.

"I don't appreciate being ordered around," she said.

Somehow I was not surprised by her tone and attitude. I smirked and repeated myself. "Come here, mate."

"Ruby," she said again. "I told you, my name is Ruby."

She sounded defiant, but she came out of the brush and walked towards me. When she got within arms' reach, I growled possessively and pulled her flush against me. I wasn't prepared for the shock my senses suffered at her touch.

"Ruby," I said reverently, feeling her quake in my arms.

My lips felt on fire as they crushed against hers. *Mate,* my wolf reminded me over and over. I had an overpowering need to possess her in every way possible. She gave entry for my tongue without hesitation, as hers darted into my mouth, swirling along my teeth. My canines immediately elongated, ready to claim her. As she brushed over the sharp points she moaned in pleasure and anticipation.

I pulled her shirt from where it was tucked neatly into her jeans. A sort of frenzy took over the second my hand grazed her bare skin. I had never given much thought to a mate, but always knew I would never deny a true mate if I was lucky enough to find her. Now here she stood. She knew it, I knew it. Nothing else in the world mattered to me in that moment but making her mine.

"Tell me you want this, Ruby," I said in a gravelly voice, barely holding myself together.

She shook at my mention of her name and stared back at me, equally dreamy-eyed and lust-filled. "Yes. Yes," she screamed, and I couldn't wait to hear those words fall from her sweet red lips again. I grinned in anticipation.

She surprised me by showing an aggressive side as she quickly disposed of my clothes, then stepped back to check me out without even blushing. From the smile that spread across her face I was certain that she liked what she saw.

"Take your clothes off, mate," I demanded. I had never felt so strong or empowered in my entire life. As the middle son of a powerful Alpha I was the most often overlooked and held the least dominance in the pack, always overshadowed by my brothers.

Ruby didn't even pause as she began a slow, sultry show of stripping for me. My mouth watered at her sight. I had never seen a more beautiful creature. Her untamed red curly hair gave her a wild appeal that I loved.

Unable to stand it anymore I closed the gap once again and devoured her with complete abandon. I didn't care about my mission. I didn't care about my brother's alliance with Westin and refusal to avenge our father's death. I didn't care about how exhausted I was physically, having gotten off the plane and walked hundreds of miles to get here. I didn't care about anything except making this beautiful creature mine. I was so single-focused on her that I gave no thought to the consequences of my actions.

Ruby

Chapter 4

Bran was a skilled lover. Thinking of him with any other woman drove my wolf to insanity. *Mine,* she growled in my head. It spurred me on to meet his passion and not back down. There was a small part of me that knew this was crazy, but it was hard to think straight with his hands on my body and his heady scent filling the air as he filled me.

I was nearly blind with desire when his teeth sunk deep into my neck and I groaned in sheer ecstasy. I needed no encouragement to follow his lead and seal a lifetime bond with this man, my one true mate.

The heightened sensitivity as our bond flared caused us both to climax together. It was the greatest feeling in the entire world, and I knew I would do anything to repeat it. I could quickly become addicted and Bran was my drug of choice.

He lovingly cradled me in his arms as we floated down from the seeming other plane of existence we'd just experienced. Neither of us spoke as I basked in the afterglow of our mating.

Mating? I sat up quickly as the reality of the situation came slamming down on me.

"What the hell have we done?" I said aloud, completely shocked.

Bran knitted his brow in frustration. "You are my one true mate, beautiful Ruby. We did what any normal mated pair would do if lucky enough to find a true mate. You are mine."

He said it like it was the most natural thing in the world, and a part of me knew that was true. I would never deny a true mate. I'd seen first-hand what that looked like in my sister Lizzy.

"Yes, but first I'd have liked to at least known a little more about you than just your name," I told him obstinately.

"I am sorry if this bothers you, but we will have a lifetime together to get to know each other." Something dark crossed his features, but he shook it off and smiled.

Reaching up, he tucked a stray hair behind my ear. I sighed. This was really happening. I was mated.

"You are now the most precious thing in the world to me. I have things to do here first, then I will take you home," he said.

I didn't think to even ask where home was. I didn't care. He had said he was a drifter, so how great could that be anyway?

"Hold up. I'm not going anywhere. I have too much counting on me here. I can't leave," I said.

"Shhh. This is not something we need to concern ourselves with right now. We can decide what's best for us later. I was planning to camp here tonight. Would you like to stay?"

"No," I said. "You can come back to my place."

"You have a house nearby?" he asked.

"Of course I do. You know you're in Collier territory, right?"

"Yes. I am hoping to speak with the Alpha tomorrow. Are you aware there is another pack nearby? I had a run in with a few of them and was forced onto Collier land. They messed up my knee pretty good, but it should heal. I'm hoping it doesn't hinder me finding work here for the season," he explained.

I rolled my eyes. "That's the Larken wolves. Sorry about that. Their Alpha was killed recently, and Luke is still struggling to control them. Many are resistant to their new Alpha's wishes and causing trouble. In some ways it's even worse now than when Jedidiah was alive," I told him.

"It would probably be best if I stayed here tonight and gave my knee more time to heal," he said regretfully.

I rolled my eyes. "I just found you. Don't think you'll get away that easily."

"There's nothing in this general area but open fields. I tried scouting ahead and this place seemed like the safest, with best coverage around."

"It's only a little over a mile back to the barns, and I have my horse. I don't just let anyone ride Cinnamon, but for you, I'll make an exception. This time," I added.

I was downplaying it. No one rode Cinnamon except me, especially since he was getting on in years now. Bran couldn't possibly understand what a big deal this was for me.

"If that will make you happy. It has been awhile since I had a real bed to sleep in."

That comment filled me with a thousand questions, but I didn't think it was the time or place to ask him. I'd take him home, maybe ask Clara to come over and check out his knee, just to be sure there was nothing wrong with it. I could use a hot shower myself and if Bran had been living off the land for several days, I was certain he could, too.

"Come on, let's get home," I told him, moving to sit up and begin gathering my clothes together.

Bran sat up next to me, kissing my shoulder. The feelings he invoked in me were indescribable. I may not know anything at all about the man, but it really didn't matter, because I would do anything to feel this sense of belonging, happiness, and need every day of my life. I pushed up to stand and quickly dressed. He did the same and gathered the few belongings he had and stuffed them into a backpack.

"That's it?" I asked.

He gave me a wry look. "I'm afraid so," he said, hesitantly. "My entire life in one bag."

"Probably a good thing," I teased, trying to lighten the melancholy that seemed to set in. "I'm high maintenance enough for the both of us."

He let out a deep full belly laugh that rumbled through his body and slammed lust back into mine. Damn, he had a sexy laugh.

I led the way out of the tree cover to where I had tied up Cinnamon. He mounted the horse first with ease. I knew I was gawking at his backside, but I doubt he minded any. I had a drop-dead gorgeous mate and I'd look all I wanted for the rest of my life.

I sat just behind the saddle, riding bareback. I knew Cinnamon wouldn't mind it much. Just before we took off, though, I heard the whine of another horse. I looked around but didn't see anything. I turned my horse to the noise to investigate. It didn't take long to identify it—Cochise.

I slowed us and slid off Cinnamon. "Cochise, where have you been, boy? Everyone's been so worried and out looking for you."

The horse whinnied and stomped his feet at my approach.

"Don't you give me that attitude, mister." I reached out and lovingly stroked his mane, and he nuzzled into my touch. "That's my good boy." I never took my eyes off Cochise, and kept the same soothing voice when I spoke to Bran. It was clear something had spooked the horse and I didn't want him to run from me. "Bran, are you okay riding solo? I've got a team out looking for this guy right now. He didn't come home last night. I can ride him back if you can manage Cinnamon okay."

"I know how to ride a horse, mate," he said sounding amused.

As I felt Cochise begin to settle, I quickly mounted him. He tried to take off on me and without a saddle I had to grab hold of his mane to keep from falling over. He then remembered just who was in charge and calmed down enough for me to get him moving.

"Well, come on then," I hollered over my shoulder. "And Cinnamon is not just some horse. He's my best friend in the entire world, so be gentle with him."

As he easily caught up to me, I glanced over and noticed he was smiling happily. Some of the edge to him seemed to have melted away, but then, Cinnamon had that effect on me, too.

We rode in silence and half an hour later the barns slowly came into view.

"Wow," Bran commented. "It's bigger than I expected."

"What is?" I asked.

"Collier," he commented.

I laughed. "Oh hon, this isn't anything. We can wash up and I'll give you the full tour if you'd like."

Something dark crossed his face again, but he nodded.

"Incoming. Two riders," Austin yelled on our approach.

"Ruby found Cochise," he announced when we got a little closer.

Half a dozen people surrounded us when we reached the barn. Before I dismounted, I barked for someone to grab me a rope.

Austin eyed Bran suspiciously. "Who the hell are you?" he finally asked. "And how the hell did you convince her to let you ride Cinnamon?"

Conlin laughed. "She must like you. No one around here's allowed to touch her horse, let alone ride him."

Bran shot me a look and I shrugged. "I warned you to be careful with him. That's my baby you're riding."

Ignoring their inquiries, when I was certain Cochise was secured, I dismounted and passed the rope to Austin. "Cool him down, then call Davidson and get his ass in here to check him over. Something out there spooked him."

"Yes, ma'am," Austin said.

Bran jumped down from Cinnamon with a hard thud next to me, then handed me his reigns. I cooed over the horse for a few minutes before Mr. Draper stepped in.

"I'll take Cinnamon and rub him down for you, Ruby girl," he said.

"You know there's no one else I trust more with him. Thank you." Knowing the excitement of our return was waning and several had moved on and gotten back to the work, I realized how rude I was being. "Mr. Draper, this is Bran. Bran, Mr. Draper oversees the horse stable here. If you need anything, he'll help you."

Bran shook his hand. "Thank you. I am Ruby's mate," he announced proudly as I broke out into a coughing fit, choking on my own spit.

I could already hear the surprised whispers beginning. I grabbed his hand, unprepared for the jolt I received from his touch, and dragged him away. Mr. Draper didn't say a word, just grinned at me and nodded.

"You can't just blurt that out around here. Oh my Lord, the entire Pack will know about this by dinnertime."

We walked around the horse stable as I led him to the dairy barn and my apartment above it.

"Ruby Red, did you really ride out and just find yourself a mate?" Austin teased.

"Shut the hell up, Austin, and mind your own business," I huffed back, never slowing my stride until we were safely in my apartment.

Bran looked around. He seemed equally frustrated and amused. "You live in a barn?"

I beamed. "Yes I do!"

"It's nice," he finally concluded.

"Thanks. I moved in here when I was seventeen and haven't looked back. I love it and since I oversee the dairy below, it's kind of perfect."

"Those people down there. They respect you," he observed.

I laughed. "Damn right they better if they want to keep their jobs."

"You're in charge?" he asked, looking more than a little shocked.

"Yes," I said slowly, wondering what he was getting at.

"But, how can that be? You're a woman," he said.

That was the first moment regret began to set in, and I realized I truly knew nothing at all about this man I'd just given my life to.

My hands were on my hips and my defenses up. "What the hell's that supposed to mean?"

He looked flustered. "I'm not meaning to offend you. It's just, that isn't how things are done where I'm from."

"You realize this is the twenty-first century, right? Equal rights and all that shit. What sort of backwoods Pack did you come from?"

His brow crinkled in frustration and he shook his head. "It doesn't matter. I was just surprised, is all."

I took a deep breath. I dealt with more than my fair share of bigots in my life. Working in a male-dominated field, it was par for the course, but I didn't like thinking my mate was one of them.

"I will never be perfect little Suzy Homemaker, Bran. I love working with the animals, and I like being in charge of things. I am stubborn to a fault. I guess there's some truth about red-heads after all, but these are things you do need to know and understand about me, because that won't change, even for you," I told him.

"Mate, I did not mean to upset you. I was only surprised and curious, is all. God chose you for me and I do not make it a habit to argue with Him," he said simply.

It didn't take long before my cell phone started sounding off. I looked down and saw Shelby's face on my screen. I rolled my eyes, knowing she'd only come over if I didn't answer it.

"What's up, Shelbs?" I asked, choosing to play it innocent. I had no doubt rumors of my mating had already reached her.

"Did you really take a mate?" she demanded, not bothering to even try to play dumb like she hadn't already heard my news.

"I did," I said.

"What?" she shrieked. "Who? When? I heard you rode out in search of Cochise and came back with a man. They say he's not a Collier wolf. What the hell is going on?"

I laughed. "Well, I guess that really does about sum it all up."

I looked over at Bran and smiled as he continued to explore my place. I could see subtle hints of him trying to mark the territory for himself. It should have pissed me off. If he were anyone else it would have, but he was my mate and it was too late to change that.

"Seriously, Ruby. I'm worried about you. Where did he come from?" she asked.

"He's a drifter looking for work, and he's my one true mate, Shelby. What was I supposed to do?"

She got quiet for a minute. "Wait, what do you mean? I mean yeah, bring him back and get to know him for sure, but you haven't done anything stupid have you?"

"Define stupid?"

I could hear the exasperation in her voice. "You haven't done anything to encourage a bond with him, have you?"

"That depends. Does sealing a bond constitute encouraging it?"

Shelby went silent on the other end. "Tell me you're kidding right now."

"Shelby, he's my one true mate. I'm not going to deny that. What did you expect me to do?"

"I don't know, maybe get to know him like a normal person! Please tell me you're kidding, Ruby. Peyton and Clara are about to head over there, we're all freaking out here."

I sighed. "Would you just calm down. No visitors right now. Bran and I have plenty to work out without you guys interfering." I was trying not to let my temper get away from me. I loved my family, but they could be a bit much at times. This was my mess to deal with and nothing they could say or do would undo what we'd done.

"Uh-oh," Shelby said.

"What now?"

"I'm over at Mom's and Austin just called and told Thomas that you brought home some foreign wolf squatting on Collier land."

"Shit!"

"You can say that again. And now Lily knows, too. I don't think I can keep those two from coming over. Thomas is really pissed."

"Great, well, shit. I don't even know what to say or do about that. Let me talk to Lily."

I heard some shuffling and then Lily came on the line. "Ruby? Girl, what the hell is going on? And why am I just now hearing about this?"

"It's not supposed to be common knowledge. I need you to calm your mate down and stay put. I will call when I'm ready to talk to you guys. For now, leave me be. Please."

"You know I can't do that," Lily snorted.

"Please, Lil. You remember what it was like when you first found your mate. You didn't exactly handle it well and didn't want anyone around to help you deal with it."

"That was different, it was Thomas!" she insisted.

"It's not different. It's called mating, and right now, I need to handle this on my own. I'll call you tonight and check in. I promise. Just buy me some time to at least get to know him first."

She sighed. "Fine. I'll do what I can, but you will check in three times a day at least. And not by text. I need to hear your voice to make sure you're still alive and well."

I rolled my eyes. "Yes, mother," I said sarcastically.

"One more thing."

"What?"

"Is he hot?"

I looked over at Bran, who was watching me closely, and I grinned. "The hottest."

27

I said goodbye and thanked her. Bran's brow crinkled in that way he seemed to do whenever something was bothering him or he was frustrated. I wasn't sure how I knew that for certain, but I did.

"Who was that?"

"My family. Word spreads fast around here. They were ready to storm the gates and come over, but I bought us a little time first. Don't want you regretting everything on day one," I joked.

He looked dark and menacing as he replied, "I will never regret you, mate."

Every time he called me "mate," it gave me a new thrill and caused goosebumps to break out across my freckled arms.

"How about I whip us up some lunch and we can just talk. You know, get to know each other, maybe."

He seemed to hesitate, but nodded, then a slow grin lightened his dark features. "You interrupted my meal earlier, so lunch sounds perfect."

"I thought I was the meal earlier," I mumbled under my breath as I headed for the kitchen. It caused another deep belly laugh to erupt from him.

Bran

Chapter 5

I had a mate. It was so surreal and the last thing I ever expected when I'd taken this mission. There weren't supposed to be secrets between mates, but I knew I could never tell her my real reasons for coming here.

I had seen up front the authority she'd carried around the stables. I had researched and learned enough about Thomas Collier to know he wouldn't trust just anyone to positions of leadership, even with stable hands. I needed to learn a hell of a lot more about my mate, and quickly.

"Can I help you with that?" I asked Ruby in the kitchen as she grilled cheese sandwiches and warmed up beef stew.

"I got it. Just make yourself at home," she insisted.

I sat down at the small kitchen table. The place was clean, neat, and organized. It was just the kind of place I would love to call home. I didn't require much in life, which meant I didn't need anything more than this small apartment with my beautiful mate.

I couldn't let myself think like that, though. I had been selfish to take Ruby as a mate so hastily. She was full of life and I was facing death. I knew that even if the plan went smoothly and I was able to get in with the Colliers and close enough to Kelsey Westin to fulfill my promise, the odds of me getting back out alive were very slim. I knew this when I'd accepted the mission. I hadn't had Ruby in my life to care about at that time.

I pushed those thoughts aside. What was done was done. I couldn't dwell on it, but I would greedily spend every second I could loving her, for as long as I was alive.

"So, you have family in the area?" I asked, trying to push past the melancholy threatening to settle in.

Ruby shot me a smile over her shoulder. "Yeah, you could definitely say that. I'm one of seven kids. My parents are still alive, too. Four of my siblings have taken mates. All have stayed in Collier except one. Two more travel a lot and are only here part of the year, but it's nice to have them around when they're home."

Seven kids. That was crazy. I had heard that Collier Pack had been very blessed with pups. Large families weren't as uncommon here as in other packs, but still. I couldn't even imagine what it must have been like growing up with so many kids.

"Where do you fall in that line?" I asked, just making conversation.

"I'm third and the middle daughter." She carried a plate of sandwiches and two steaming bowls of soup on a tray, placing them on the table before me.

My stomach rumbled in anticipation and my mouth watered at the smells filling the room.

"That must have been something. I can't even imagine."

"Do you have siblings?"

"Two brothers," I confessed. "I am also the middle child. My parents are no longer with us." The darkness threatened to consume me as I fought back my need to avenge their deaths. If Ruby noticed, she didn't comment.

"No sisters?"

"No," I said, quickly taking a sandwich and stuffing my mouth full. I hoped it would stall the conversation so we could pick up with less personal things. I didn't want to lie to her, but I had to protect the mission, even from my mate. The less questions about my family and Pack, the better.

"Well, you're lucky then. I love my sisters, but they can be quite invasive. I know I've been guilty of it with them as well, even if it was good intentions. But I hate knowing they could storm the place and barge in at any second."

"The door is locked, right? They can't just come in," I said.

Ruby scoffed. "I've never locked that door even once. What's the point?"

I scowled. "Ruby, you've been a single woman living alone, or I assume so at least. It's not safe to leave the door unlocked so just anyone could wander in."

I hadn't seen any signs of a roommate or man in her life. If she had another man in her life, she wouldn't have bonded with me. Would she? Another reminder that I knew absolutely nothing about my mate. While the desire to share things with her was already there, I knew I had to be vigilant at keeping my mouth shut lest I ruin the mission. I couldn't sway my focus, not even for Ruby.

"Your safety is very important to me. That's one thing that's going to change quickly," I assured her, getting up to walk over to the front door and lock it. When I got there, I saw that the lock required a key. "Where's the key?"

Ruby laughed. "Honestly, I have no idea. I told you there's no concern here for that. I'm not sure that old lock has had a key since I moved in here."

I frowned. "When was that?"

"The day I turned seventeen, so pushing ten years now."

I groaned. "I'll find a hardware store tomorrow."

"You'd do best to just order it online if you're going to be all pigheaded about it. Doubt our local hardware store even bothers carrying them. No one locks anything around here. The Pack protects their own, so there's no need," she insisted.

"I'm not willing to risk your safety on that," I told her stubbornly.

Much to my relief, she just laughed but didn't argue with me.

The remainder of lunch was steered towards lighter conversations. Ruby decided we just needed to get to know each other, and at first I feared what that would entail and how much I'd have to lie to her, but it wasn't deep soul-searching questions she was after, it was the simple things in life: What was my favorite color? What kind of foods did I like? How old was I? When was my birthday? With these basic questions, I relaxed and even let my guard down a little as I answered each one honestly.

When she confessed her biggest pet peeve in life was being lied to or kept in the dark about things, even for her own good, I felt a physical stab of pain in my chest. When I agreed to take the mission to kill Elena, I was filled with spite and needed revenge for my parents' deaths. I was so consumed with hate and anger that I couldn't see straight. I had justified every decision that got me here without any remorse, until now.

Though it had been quick and crazy, and I was only beginning to get to know my mate, bonding with Ruby had instantly filled the hole in my heart that I hadn't been aware was even there. She had made me laugh several times, something I couldn't remember having done since childhood. And I felt more relaxed than I ever had before, like an invisible weight had been lifted from my shoulders.

Sheltered away from the rest of the world in this apartment where only Ruby and I existed made it difficult to remember I was in enemy territory. The Collier family was as much my enemy as the Westins; I needed to keep that at the forefront of my thoughts and keep that torch of hatred for them alive and burning brightly.

Later in the afternoon Ruby's phone rang again and I heard her decline a dinner invitation. She hung up the phone and stared at the screen for a minute.

"My mom," she finally said. "I know I just disappointed her and everyone's excited to meet you, but is it really so bad that I just want one day alone with you?"

I shook my head, surprised by her question. "No, my beautiful mate. Today is our day. There will be plenty of time to meet your family later." *And your Alpha,* I thought without saying.

I briefly wondered if perhaps Ruby's family had connections to Thomas Collier, then immediately admonished the thought. Under no circumstances would I use my new mate for political gain or assistance in this mission.

"Would you like to go for a drive?" she asked.

I smiled and nodded. "That would be nice. All I have seen of Collier territory so far was a bit of the fields and a glimpse of the stables and barns."

"Well, you can get up in the morning and get a look at those up close, but how about a drive around town? I'll call in an order at the diner and I can swing in and pick it up on our way home. The menu's on the fridge."

I looked it over while Ruby disappeared into the next room. She returned a few minutes later in fresh clothes. Her button-down shirt stopped just above the peak of her breasts and I knew I was staring.

She smiled, knowing she was driving me crazy. I hadn't had her since our initial bonding that morning. The thought of riding in a car with her seemed like a torturous plan when we could simply retire to the bedroom for the night. Who needed food anyway?

My stomach rumbled loudly, reminding me I did. Coming here with only about fifty dollars in my pocket and the clothes on my back to look humble and beg for work meant I'd been starving myself for the last week in preparation to have little or nothing to eat before that first paycheck.

It was necessary to the plan. I had to infiltrate the Colliers and get in good with the Alpha. I needed to be invited to accompany him to Westin Pack. Security there was too tight otherwise. It was my only hope of getting close enough to Kelsey to kill her.

I hadn't planned on Ruby as part of all of this. I truly hoped that mating her would not affect the plan, at least not in a negative way. As I looked over the menu and the prices, I knew I would have to count on her to provide meals for a while. I hated that more than anything, and would pay her back every penny, but my need to eat was going to override my stubborn pride.

As if sensing my hesitation, Ruby said, "Look. I know we haven't talked about a lot of the important stuff, but you need to know that we have money. Lots of it. Order whatever you want."

It warmed my heart to hear her say "we."

"That isn't my money, that's yours. I do have money, Ruby, it's just tied up and not accessible to me at the moment," I said honestly. I couldn't explain it to her, but I needed my mate to know I would care for her. Everything I had would go to her when I died, and she'd know the truth. I couldn't let myself think about that though.

"Bran, you're my mate. What's mine is yours. Period. We can afford to grab dinner out tonight. We can afford to eat every meal out every day, but I don't make a habit of it, which only means it accumulates faster than I know what to do with it. I know you're hungry. I don't know how long you've been on your own, but I can tell it's been a while. I can literally hear your stomach growling. If you don't want to choose dinner, fine, I will pick it for you."

I was truly humbled like I'd never been before. Taking a mate so quickly upon meeting her was a rash decision, and probably the best thing I'd ever done in my life. It hadn't even been a full day, but I knew Ruby was good all the way to her very soul. I didn't deserve someone like her, but I would selfishly hold on to her for as long as I possibly could.

I knew to fully penetrate the Collier Pack I would need to spend months, maybe even years, getting into position to make my move. That knowledge had almost kept me from her, but looking at the gorgeous redhead before me, it didn't feel like it would be long enough.

"Steak, rare; baked potato, no sour cream; and green beans," I finally said.

"Now, that wasn't so hard, was it?" Ruby asked, leaning in to kiss me as she passed, still flitting around the apartment getting ready.

"Should I be cleaning up for this outing?"

Ruby laughed. "You're fine, unless you want to."

I considered that for a moment. I desperately needed a shower, but I needed food more. "I do want a shower, but I want food more," I told her.

"I was figuring as much. Come on," she said, grabbing her purse and heading for the door.

I followed her down the stairs and outside where she jumped into a large Ford pickup truck. I climbed into the passenger seat next to her.

"Are those the only clothes you have?" she asked without judgement in her voice.

I shook my head. "I have a spare in my backpack," I confessed.

She seemed to be sizing me up then nodded to herself. "Gage is about your size. I'll call Clara and see if we can borrow a few things until we can go shopping. Rumors are too wild right now to really go out in public," she said.

I wondered briefly if I embarrassed her. I looked down at my dusty clothes. They weren't ripped or torn or anything. I didn't feel like I looked like the drifter I was trying to portray at least.

"Oh it's not you," she said like she was once again reading my mind. "It's them. Trust me. All of them."

We drove around in silence for a while. The only time she really spoke was to point out one place or another. Eventually she began to relax again and tell me funny stories about the different places she was showing me, or tales from her childhood. She even confessed she had always been a bit of a hellion, though she rebelled against her parents and life in general less than her siblings.

"Knowing my entire life what I wanted to do helped that, I think," she confessed.

"What was it you always wanted to do?" I asked curiously.

"Stay here, work the farm, take care of the animals, basically be a cowgirl. It's all I've ever wanted."

I smiled. "And here you are, living your dream."

"Yes I am," she said proudly.

There was an awkward silence that filled the cab. It was normal for a male to bring his mate back to his Pack to live. How would Ruby do back in Bulgaria in a small rebel Pack? In some ways I thought the fire within her would shine brightly if she came to believe in the fight my Pack was created for. On the other hand, that was no place for my mate.

Ruby

Chapter 6

Sometimes Bran got this dark look in his eyes and I'd give anything to know what he was thinking. He was doing that again now. I tried to keep my stories light and fun. It was clear something was weighing heavily on him, and I didn't think that had anything to do with me.

I still had a million questions I wanted answers to, but I'd made good progress at least in getting to know him for only our first day together. I didn't feel like I had a complete stranger sitting next to me anymore.

If we were going to stop by Clara's tonight, I needed to give her the heads-up. At the next stop sign, I grabbed my phone and dialed her number before turning left and heading into town. So far I'd only shown him the country side of Collier.

"Hello?" Clara's voice came through the phone.

"Hey, Clara. I have a big favor to ask," I said, like there wasn't anything truly important I needed to share.

"Hey, Ruby. Are you okay? Mom's worried sick about you. The entire Pack is talking about some stranger you brought home. Thomas is livid knowing a foreign wolf was squatting on his land, but mostly he's just really worried about you and Lily insists everyone needs to leave you alone."

"She's the best!" I exclaimed. "Go ahead and ask your questions quickly," I said with a sigh, knowing we needed to get past that part so I could beg for clothes.

"You know what?" Clara said. "Lily told me he's your true mate. And I know how insane that was for me and Gage. I can't imagine having to deal with that under the scrutiny of not just the family, but the entire Pack. Take a few days, or weeks even, and get things sorted out. If you need someone to talk to or anything at all, you know I'm here for you."

I felt the tension ease from my shoulders. I knew I could always count on Clara, that's why I called her to begin with. "Actually there is something I need. Bran only has a few things with him, and he could really use some clothes to get through the next few days. I'm just not ready to stroll into town with him just yet, for all the reasons you just mentioned. He's about Gage's size so I was wondering if we could borrow a few things."

"Of course you can. Gage literally had the clothes on his back when we met, so I totally get it. Do you want me to put together a few things and bring them over?"

"We're actually out now. I'm giving him the grand tour of Collier. We're about to head downtown and then I'm going to call in an order at Kate's. Thought we could swing by while we're over your way," I said hopefully.

"Absolutely. Do we get to meet him?"

"Maybe. I think that will be okay."

She gave a little squeal of excitement. "I'll have a bag packed and ready for you."

"Okay, give us about fifteen minutes."

We drove down Collier and I stopped in front of my parents' house. "That's the Alpha House," I told him.

"I'm going to have to go there soon and check in officially.'

"I know, just not tonight," I said. I wasn't ready to open that can of worms.

I circled around through the town, then drove over to Clara's. Before I had the truck in park, she and Gage were standing on the porch excitedly watching.

"Should I come?" Bran asked.

"Yeah, you might as well. You're going to have to meet everyone eventually anyway. Let me call in our dinner first. That will give us a get out of dodge excuse if they try to keep us too long," I joked. In truth, we were here because I knew Clara respected boundaries better than any of my other siblings.

Peyton answered as I called Kate's Diner. "Kate's Diner, Peyton speaking. What can I do for you?"

"Hey Pey, it's Ruby. I need to place an order for pick up."

"Ruby? You've been the talk of the night around here. Give me your order, and then phone me when you get here, and I'll run it out to you. You and that stranger of yours is the latest obsession right now."

I groaned. "Thanks for the tip, Peyton. Give me the largest steak you have in house, rare, with a baked potato and green beans. Then I'll take my usual," I said.

"You got it. One large steak dinner, baked potato, and green beans, and a meatloaf with carrots and French fries," she said, reading it back to me.

"Sounds perfect. About how long will that take?"

"Pretty busy tonight, give me twenty."

"You're the best. Love you," I said hanging up.

Bran raised an eyebrow at me. "You say 'I love you' to the diner waitress?"

"Yes, doesn't everyone?" I asked, feeling snarky. I knew he didn't understand and burst out laughing at the strange look he was giving me. "Peyton's one of my sisters," I finally told him.

"That makes so much more sense," he said, looking relieved.

"Now come on and meet Clara and Gage."

We got out of the car and met around the front of it. He took my hand in his, linking our fingers together. I relaxed at his touch. I couldn't believe how nervous I was, introducing him to part of my family.

"Hey," Clara said when we reached the porch as she hugged me. "You holding up okay?"

I smiled and nodded. "Sure am. Clara, Gage, this is Bran, my mate."

Bran shook hands with Gage and offered a one-armed hug to Clara as he never let go of my hand.

"Would you like to come in for a few minutes?" Clara asked hopefully.

"We have twenty minutes, then Pey is gonna smuggle dinner out for us, as apparently we're the talk of the town." I rolled my eyes and groaned.

"Since when did you ever mind being the center of attention?" Clara teased as we walked into their home and took seats on the couch.

"I know. This is just different," I said, and she and Gage shared a look like they truly understood.

"So Bran, what brings you to Collier?" Gage asked. He was just making small talk, but I felt Bran stiffen next to me.

"Work. Ran into some shifters over in Boise and they were telling me that there may be seasonal work around here. I figured it was worth a shot."

I didn't know how I knew for certain, but I knew that wasn't entirely the truth. I gave him the benefit of the doubt and figured he was just embarrassed about his circumstances. I didn't care. He was my mate and I had more than enough to provide for the both of us.

"I'm sure that can be arranged. There's always plenty to do around the farm," Gage said.

I had been a little skeptical at first, but had grown to love Gage in time. He had plenty of his own baggage from his past, but he was a good guy and he was good for my sister.

We chatted for a bit, losing track of time until my phone dinged with a new text from Peyton.

"Looks like time's up. When things settle down a little, I'll take this guy shopping and return your things. Thanks for letting him borrow them," I told Gage as I hugged him bye.

Gage stiffened a little in surprise and quickly shot a look over to Bran.

"What?" I asked, not one to just let things like that slide.

"He didn't growl," Clara said curiously. "Most mating males are super protective and can't stand for their mates to be near another male, let alone hug one."

Bran shrugged. "Gage is already happily mated and sealing the bond helps control that a lot. My wolf doesn't find him a threat and neither do I."

Clara's eyes were huge as she grabbed my head and twisted it to one side. The mark of our bond was clearly visible.

"When did you meet? How long has this been going on?" she demanded.

"This morning," I told her, trying not to make a big deal of it.

"And you already sealed your bond? Are you crazy? You don't know anything about him."

"I know the only thing that matters," I said, taking Bran's hand and moving closer to his side. "He's my one true mate, and I'm not going to screw that up by fighting it."

"Smart man," Gage said admirably. "Boy, do I wish I'd had the balls to just seal our bond the second we met, but even that thought scared me shitless."

Clara elbowed him in the ribs.

"Well, I guess I'm happy for you. You seem like a great guy, Bran, but you better take damn good care of my sister," she said.

I tried not to laugh. Clara was the smallest of all of my siblings and the most laid back. Very little riled her up and it was always funny to watch when something did.

"We really have to go," I insisted. "I'll call you tomorrow."

I ushered Bran to the truck, and then drove over to meet Peyton.

"Clara seemed surprised we would bond so quickly."

I snorted. "Yeah, well, three of my sisters have bonded mates now, as well as my brother. They all fought their mating. I swore if I was ever lucky enough to find you, I wouldn't. It's really that simple."

"I'm glad," he said sincerely.

I parked the truck at the back of the diner and leaned over to kiss him. A knock on the window startled me.

"Your truck was spotted when you pulled up. Here's your food. Square up later, I put it on your tab for now." Peyton looked around. "The curious are about to descend, so you probably want to get out of here."

"Thanks, Pey," I said, taking the bags from her and passing them to Bran.

"Hi, I'm Peyton," she said to Bran.

"Bran. It's nice to meet you."

"You, too. Now get out of here and call me tomorrow," she ordered.

Peyton usually only got assertive in the kitchen, but since she'd taken the job as head chef at Kate's Diner, that bossy side of her had been popping up in all facets of her life. I was proud to see it.

"How much food did you order?" Bran asked when we arrived back to the apartment. "This thing weighs a ton."

I shrugged. I had told Peyton to give me the biggest steak they had. I thought Bran could use the meat. He was going to need his strength to keep up with me. I grinned evilly at the thought.

I pulled out plates and silverware and set them on the table. He unpacked the food and stepped back, staring in shock at the enormous porterhouse before him.

"What is that?"

I laughed. "Your dinner. You wanted steak, right?"

"Not the entire cow. That thing must have cost a fortune."

I shrugged. "I don't really care how much it costs. I told Pey to give you the biggest they had. Wolf shifters require meat. Lots of it. We live on a cattle ranch, that's not an uncommon meal around here. Eat up."

I grabbed two beers and set them on the table before I sunk into my chair and dug into my own dinner. All the portions were large at the diner. Our kind required an excessive amount of food, especially meat.

Bran finally dug in and moaned as he sunk his teeth into the first bite.

"Keep that up and you really won't be finishing this meal," I warned.

He gulped then grinned back at me. We ate quickly. Despite his protests, he polished off every bite of food. I got up to clear the table as he went to take a shower. When I was done and the last dish was put away, I sat down on the couch trying not to listen to the water raining down from the shower where my mate stood naked and probably wanting.

I had never been shy with my sexuality, and I wasn't about to start now. I quickly stripped, dropping my clothes into the hamper outside the bathroom and walked in. Bran didn't notice my intrusion at first. As he turned and leaned his back against the shower wall, I saw he was a little busy. A pang of irrational jealousy shot through me at the sight of him stroking himself.

When our eyes met, he didn't break his stride.

"I could have taken care of that for you," I said, stepping into the shower.

"It's been a long, crazy day. I didn't want to assume," he admitted.

I dropped to my knees and took over to finish what he'd started.

"*Po dyavolite!*" he swore as his legs began to shake.

I kissed my way up his body till our lips met and I swirled my tongue with his, loving the taste of him.

I pulled back to smile at him, pushing wet hair from his forehead. "I'm your mate, you're free to always assume," I said.

He growled, kissing me back passionately. He turned us and pressed my back up against the shower wall. "Mine," he said, causing chills to break out across my body despite the hot water pummeling down on me.

Between the headiness of the bond and the heightened sensations of the hot water, my body was instantly on fire with desire.

He didn't disappoint either as he cupped my breasts and nearly drove me mad with his touch. I came hard, twice, once by his hand and then by his mouth before my legs felt like Jell-O and could no longer hold me upright.

Bran turned off the water and lifted me into his arms, carrying me out of the room and into my bedroom. He laid me gently down on the bed and climbed up to hover over me. I didn't think I had anything left in me to give. Then he kissed me sweetly and nudged my knees apart. Just like that, my body came alive again.

This time being with Bran was very different. It wasn't the hurried frenzy of our initial mating, nor the exploratory fun of the shower. This was a slow timeless dance between a man and a woman who cared about each other.

It was far too early to say we loved each other. We were still getting to know each other, but this wasn't just sex either; it was more of a promise of so much more. We never broke eye contact, even when my building orgasm threatened to close them. I forced myself to keep the connection that took my breath away and stirred something deep inside of me.

He groaned and shook in my arms, as I watched his eyes flicker in differing shades of green and brown. There was so much more to this man hidden in those eyes. I let go and let my orgasm take me to a higher plane as my muscles contracted and my toes curled.

As I floated down from my high, Bran repositioned us in bed, pulling the covers over us and tucking me safely into his side. We didn't say a word. There wasn't a need for them as I drifted off to sleep, thinking back through our perfect day together.

Waking the next morning was a bit surreal. I had never let a guy stay over before, and I certainly hadn't ever stayed over at one of their places. Sex was fun and one thing but waking up in Bran's arms was about the most intimate thing I'd ever experienced, and awkward.

There was definitely something to the whole "morning after" thing. Fortunately, he was still asleep, and I wiggled out of bed and took a shower to begin my day.

As I was in the kitchen grabbing some breakfast, Bran woke up and stumbled out of the bedroom, looking groggy and like sex on a stick. My mouth watered and I struggled to breathe normally. Lust filled me and I couldn't bring myself to speak or even turn to leave.

The phone rang and my hand was shaking as I answered it. "Hello?"

"Hey Ruby, it's Clay. I heard the good news. Congratulations," he said.

"Uh, for what?" I asked, my head still in a daze, drooling over the Adonis that was now stretching and showing off new muscles I'd had yet to explore.

"I heard you found your mate. That's kind of a big deal."

"Uh, yeah, yup, big deal," I said, unable to suddenly form a coherent sentence.

"Well, relax and take it easy. Spend time with your mate. I'll hold down the fort for the next few days. I have to make a run in three days, but you can take off the next two for yourself if you want. I know, you're the boss, not me, I'm just offering."

"Uh, yeah, thanks, Clay. I really appreciate that. And I think I'll take you up on it," I said.

I wasn't sure who was more shocked, him or me. I rarely took time off from work, and never for truly personal reasons. I didn't even care that they all knew why. I selfishly wanted more time with my mate and just then, nothing else mattered.

For the next two days we didn't even leave the apartment as we learned everything there was to know about each other.

On the day I was to return to work, Clay called and said his run had been pushed back another day, giving me one final day with just Bran. While I was growing to love having him around, I was also beginning to go stir-crazy and was more than ready to return to work. There were little things about living with someone that just grated on my nerves. It wasn't just me. I could see him cringe each time I drank straight from the milk carton. It had always just been me, my milk. I didn't need to worry about what others thought because no one else was drinking it but me.

Now there was this "us" and I knew I had to change some of my habits, but it wasn't going to be easy and I was stubborn to a fault, so it was in my nature to push back against those things. We hadn't exactly argued about anything, but I felt like we were headed to a boiling point where we would be soon.

"Bran, there's a hamper right next to your dirty clothes. For the love of all things holy, just put them in the hamper. How hard is that?"

"Sorry, Ruby. I'll try to remember."

Gah, it was those little things that were going to drive me insane. *Tomorrow life would return to some semblance of normal*, I kept reminding myself.

There was a pounding at the door.

"Ruby, open up," I heard Thomas yell.

Bran immediately went on the defense, but I waved him off.

"I got this," I assured him.

I opened the door, but refused to let him in. "What are you doing here?"

"This is the fourth day, Ruby. Don't you think he should at least talk to the Alpha?"

"Five days, Thomas. He has five days to sort that out. I took a few days off so we could spend time together, so back off. I don't care who you are, you're still my little brother and you aren't going to barge into my home demanding shit!"

"You're infuriating, you know that," he yelled back. "Tomorrow's your fifth day. You can't hide him forever."

"I'm not hiding, jackass!" I yelled to his retreating back as he headed down the stairs. I slammed the door shut with all the frustrations that had been building over the last few days.

"That was your brother?"

"Yes."

"He's right, you know. It's disrespectful that I haven't introduced myself and sought permission to be in Collier territory yet. I thought you'd be returning to work today and had planned on seeking a meeting with your Alpha to get that sorted."

"Really? You want to see the Alpha now? You couldn't have told me that before I yelled at him?" I could see the confusion on Bran's face and it dawned on me that I'd never mentioned my family in regards to our status here. Did he really not know Thomas was my brother? I walked over to the window and opened it. Thomas was talking to Lily by his truck just below. "Thomas, get your ass back up here already. He wants to talk to the Alpha," I said sarcastically.

"Can I come too?" Lily hollered up.

"You better," I yelled back down.

Bran

Chapter 7

Reality was slowly sinking in. Ruby wasn't just a Collier wolf, she was a Collier.

"Thomas Collier is your brother?" I asked in disbelief.

"Yeah. I thought you knew that. I'm Ruby Collier," she said.

"And you never mentioned that?"

"Sure I did. Didn't I?" She shrugged. "I thought you knew. Does it matter?"

Yes, I wanted to say. It mattered a lot to my mission. I had vowed not to use Ruby in any way, and yet, just by mating her, I had. It escalated my position here and gave me a direct line to the Alpha.

"It doesn't. I'm just surprised is all," I finally managed to tell her, still in shock from the bomb she'd just dropped on me.

The door flung open and there he stood. The young Alpha I was planning to use and manipulate, Ruby's brother. It made me sick to my stomach just thinking about it. This man was supposed to be my enemy, not my brother-in-law. This changed everything.

Thomas Collier is Ruby's brother. That one thought kept playing on repeat in my brain. There he stood, a real-life version of the pictures I'd studied. I had researched his family extensively. I knew he had sisters. Why hadn't I noted their names? Probably because I was focused solely on Elizabeth, who I knew went by Lizzy, and Madelyn, whom they called Maddie.

46

Why those two only? Because they were both mated into Westin Pack with strong alliances and easy access to my target. I hadn't thought the remaining sisters would be all that beneficial and had never even entertained the idea of mating into the family.

I had always known I would only ever bond with my true mate. It didn't matter the mission, a true mate was simply too precious a find and I knew I was a lucky son-of-a-bitch for finding mine, but I really wish Thomas wasn't her brother.

Once Thomas was fully in the room, I snapped out of my shock. I walked up and bowed my head to him humbly. I had an Alpha. I would not bare my neck and fully submit to another, but I could show humility and submission to his position.

"Hi, I'm Bran," I said, straightening and offering him my hand.

"Thomas," he said. "What are you doing in my territory?"

"Thomas," Ruby growled, but he brushed her off.

I couldn't help but chance a look over to my feisty mate and grin.

"I heard you might be hiring for help heading into spring," I said, just as I had rehearsed.

"And that just gives you the right to trespass on my land?"

I knew this was all a formality and had been expecting it.

"No, sir. My humblest apologies for that. I was careful to avoid your territory when I got to the area but was pushed onto it during a minor altercation with what I believe Ruby refers to as a Larken wolf. I meant no disrespect and I was coming to see you the next day, but, well, I got a little shock and priorities changed quickly. You have a mate, I'm certain you understand what I'm talking about."

I saw him glance over at the woman that had come in with him. Lily Westin. I knew who she was from the pictures I had memorized when preparing to come here.

"Just because you're mating my sister doesn't mean I'll treat you any differently," Thomas said.

"Oh please, stop with the macho crap," Ruby said.

I shook my head. "I wouldn't have it any other way."

Thomas grinned and nodded. "Glad to hear it. Welcome to Collier Pack. I'm certain we can find something for you to do around here."

The thing that threw me off-guard the most was that I instantly liked Thomas Collier. I had prepared to hate him. On paper he was little more than an overentitled pompous ass, a spoiled little rich kid who was handed the title of Alpha much too soon, yet there was something commanding about him. I felt like I was in the presence of a truly powerful Alpha.

"Thank you," I said sincerely.

"Now, tell me what your intentions are with my sister."

I blanched for a minute. I knew there were still packs out there that held to the strict antiquated notion that mates, even true mates, needed to be vetted first and approved by the pack. I didn't know where Collier Pack stood on this. Concern crept in as I looked to Ruby for guidance.

Ignoring him entirely, Ruby introduced me to Lily, Thomas's mate.

"Hello. It's nice to meet you," I said, still feeling a little overwhelmed by the situation I found myself in.

"It's really great to meet you, too. Now, answer his question. We've heard the rumors that you two are mating, but what do you intend to do with that? Will you be sticking around? Will you be transferring allegiance to Collier? Are you planning to bond with her?" Lily asked one question after another until my head was spinning.

"We're already bonded. I plan to stick around a while. We'll decide in time where we're supposed to be and what Pack we should live in," I said truthfully.

Lily squealed and turned to Ruby. "You what? And you didn't call me? Why didn't you tell anyone?"

Ruby shrugged and blushed. "It's still very new. I know, Clara was just as surprised."

"Wait, you told Clara before us?" Thomas demanded.

Ruby shrugged again and tried to give an innocent look. "I didn't want to just show up in town with all the rumors flying around, so I borrowed some clothes from Gage until I can get Bran out shopping for his own."

"You don't have any clothes?" Lily asked.

It was my turn to shrug. "I have enough to get by, just not enough by her standards."

Lily laughed. "Okay, fair enough."

Thomas put his arm around Ruby as she leaned into him. The gesture set my wolf on edge and I bit back a growl. He hadn't reacted that way with Gage, but now did with her brother?

Thomas laughed as I started to apologize. "Don't worry about it. My wolf is very dominant and has that effect on others. That's the number one reason my father stepped down so soon to hand the reigns over to me."

I had never considered that as a reason before. As news had travelled to Bulgaria regarding the situation in Collier Pack, it had been assumed that Zach Collier, the previous Alpha, had been ill or injured to step down and give it over to a pup. If what Thomas was saying was true, then that wasn't the case at all. He'd stepped down knowing that his son was stronger and wouldn't submit for much longer.

That also meant that the assumptions that Collier Pack was weak and would be easily infiltrated was very wrong. If anything, the only weakness I saw in the man before me was his love of family. It gutted me that I was inadvertently capitalizing on that fact, but Ruby was my one true mate. We were bonded now and there was nothing I could do to change that.

"What pack are you from anyway?" Thomas asked as he motioned for me to sit and the girls headed off to the kitchen.

"It's hardly what you'd call a pack anymore. I'm from a small pack in Indiana," I said, using my cover story.

"That one that aligned with the Bulgarians against the Westins? I thought they were all but wiped out."

I pursed my lips at the mention of the battle that had killed my father. "Like I said, a pretty small pack now. I hope that doesn't bother you. I wasn't involved in that battle and you can't help who your family is," I said truthfully, thinking of my older brother and how if he had only stepped up and avenged our father's death, it wouldn't have fallen to me to do it.

But then, I wouldn't be here right now, and I wouldn't have met Ruby. That thought felt like a sword slicing through my chest. I couldn't afford to let myself feel anything more than the bond for her. I'd be leaving eventually, and I couldn't risk her coming along. I was already ashamed for how she would feel when the truth came out.

"That's true. I'm sure that must have been hard. I honestly hadn't realized anyone had survived."

I shrugged. I didn't think anyone had either which made for an easy cover story and no way to validate it. "The few of us that did, dispersed. I've been travelling for a while now, on my own. Ran into some shifters around Boise and they told me about this place and that I may be able to find work."

"Well, I'm glad they did," Thomas said. "I heard Ruby was returning to work in the morning, so I'll come by tomorrow and we can talk in detail."

I didn't get why he was being so nice to me. I hadn't been certain how he would take me claiming to be from the Indiana Pack after the mess that went down with the Westins and the fact that they had aligned with us to fight them. It had been a gamble and I thought I would have to spend time proving myself to be trustworthy, but it was the only Pack I could think of that wouldn't cause him to immediately validate my claim. Instead, was that compassion I saw in his eyes? Maybe a little sympathy? Did he really feel sorry for me and my made-up situation?

"Tomorrow sounds good," I said. Nothing with Thomas was going as I had envisioned.

"You really bonded with my sister?" he finally asked.

I pulled back the collar of my shirt to show him my mating mark.

Thomas gave a low whistle and shook his head. "I know I'm the baby of the family, but it's crazy watching all my sisters pair off with mates. That's four now. Only two more to go."

"I'm sure they thought it just as odd to watch you bond with Lily."

He grinned. "Yeah, that one shocked us all. I wasn't exactly her favorite person. At least it doesn't seem that Ruby fought your bond. That's uncharacteristic of these Collier girls. I think you two have had the easiest mating I've ever heard of. How's it going?"

I looked at Ruby and my brow wrinkled.

"That good?" Thomas asked.

I laughed. "Everything is fine, great even. Ruby is wonderful, but sometimes she can be a little opinionated, stubborn—or perhaps pigheaded would be the correct word."

Thomas burst out laughing. "Well at least you caught on to that quickly. She's also very territorial and likes things a certain way."

I rolled my eyes. I had already learned that lesson, too. God forbid so much as one little sock missed the hamper.

Ruby and Lily came back into the living room. Ruby took the last spot on the couch next to me while Lily sat on a chair across from us.

"You playing nice, little brother?" she warned.

Thomas gave her an innocent look. "What? We were just getting to know each other."

"We should probably go and give these two some alone time. Ruby's back to the grind tomorrow and the real world will come crashing in quickly," Lily reminded us.

I couldn't bring myself to admit I was happy for it. Ruby was great, but we'd spent the last three days doing nothing but talking and making love. We hadn't left the apartment since the first night I arrived and my wolf and I were both getting a little stir crazy. I needed some space, and a break from my mate. I wished I had someone to ask if that was normal or a sign of trouble. In all my adult life I had lived alone, so this was a definite learning curve for me.

We said goodbye to Thomas and Lily. As soon as the door shut, Ruby rounded on me.

"I'm sorry about that. They can be a little much. I hope Thomas didn't grill you too badly. We were all pretty brutal to Gage when he first arrived. I may have been the main cause of that. Karma can be a real bitch and I just hope they don't gang up on you like we did him."

"Do I even want to ask?"

"No, probably not," Ruby admitted.

"Life with you will never be boring, will it, mate?"

She wrapped her arms around my neck and kissed my lips softly. "No, it definitely won't be," she admitted.

Ruby

Chapter 8

The next morning, I awoke with the sun before my alarm clock even went off. I had wanted to show Bran around and let him see what it was that I do, but he was still sleeping soundly, and I'd heard Thomas mention he would come by and talk to him about work today, so I left the bed as quietly as I could and headed straight for the bathroom.

After a quick shower and an even faster breakfast, I was ready to head out the door. I walked my short commute down the stairs and was surprised to see Clay already checking on the cows.

"Good morning," he said as I approached.

"What are you doing here? I thought you had a run to make today."

"I do, but we're not leaving until ten, so I thought I'd get a jumpstart on the day. You ready to return?"

"Yes, I was more than ready yesterday," I mumbled under my breath.

"What? Life isn't all peachy in Ruby-land with the new mate?" Clay asked.

I sighed. "Bran is wonderful. It'll just take some getting used to having someone up in my space all the time."

"Poor guy," Clay said solemnly.

I punched him in the arm. "Poor guy? What the hell's that supposed to mean?"

Clay gave me a look. "Ruby. I love you, you know that, but you are a stubborn bitch, not to mention a micro-managing control freak. That poor guy doesn't stand a chance."

I frowned. I had no comeback to that because we both knew it was true.

I chose instead to just change the subject. "How're my babies? Everyone doing okay? Any issues I should be aware of?"

Clay shook his head. "Nope. Nothing exciting to report. Mellie's still very pregnant. I would have sent someone after you if she'd started to go into labor, but she gets closer every day."

I smiled, grateful I hadn't missed the delivery of the twins. I never missed a new calf being born.

"Hey, thanks for holding down the fort for me," I told Clay.

He nodded, not one to push the subject. As Austin entered the barn, I knew that was a whole different story.

"Ruby Red, why I never."

"Never what, Austin?" I asked.

He gave me a boyish grin that I'm sure would have some ladies go weak in the knees, but all it did was piss me off. "Why, I never thought in a million years you'd fall so quickly. Look at that, you're not even bothering to hide the mark."

My hands flew to my neck where Bran's mating mark was, and I knew my cheeks burned as red as my hair.

"Wow, I've never seen you turn quite that red," Clay commented. I gave him a shove with my free hand.

"So the rumors are clearly true. And I guess it's too late now to point out the obvious, like what the hell is he doing here? Guy just shows up in our territory and you instantly mate him. What the hell, Ruby? You're smarter than that," Austin said.

The truth was, I understood where he was coming from. I would be concerned and maybe even a little pissed if anyone I cared about had done the same.

I sighed. "He's my one true mate. Why fight it?"

"Oh shit. You're serious? Wow. That's crazy, Ruby. I mean, what are the odds?"

I shrugged. "I don't know. I think we were both a little shocked by it all. It's been a strange few days and if you two goons don't mind, I'd like to just get back to my normal routine."

They were both quiet for once, but I didn't miss the shared look between them. Choosing to ignore them, I set about my day, finding peace in the mundane and familiar.

When all the chores were done for the day and the evening crew was arriving to settle the animals in for the night, I actually felt a little more like my normal self. I headed upstairs, surprised to find Bran gone. I wasn't expecting equal parts disappointment and relief.

I stripped and jumped in the shower. As I headed for the kitchen, I saw a note he'd left that he was having dinner with Thomas to discuss jobs. I wasn't sure if that was an invitation to join them or not as he'd listed when and where they'd be. I decided it was just Bran being thoughtful and letting me know, and I wasn't going to disturb them. It would be good for two of the most important men in my life to spend time together.

Though I had missed my mate throughout the day, it had also been great having a break from him. What did that say about our relationship? Was that normal?

I needed someone to talk to, quick. I headed outside and jumped in my truck. When I pulled in at Clara's. I hesitated because I hadn't even thought to call her ahead of time. Before I could talk myself into turning around and just going to the diner and seeing if Peyton was working, Clara stepped out on her porch and walked over to me.

"Hey Ruby, what's up?" she asked, sounding concerned.

I frowned. "Can we talk?"

"Lizzy's here. She and Cole just got back in from Westin this morning. Come on in."

"Oh, never mind. I didn't mean to interrupt your evening. Bran's having dinner with Thomas tonight."

"Great, I'll call Lily and tell her to come on over and we'll make a sisters' night of it then. Gage is helping Cole with a pipe that sprung a leak while they were away. The place is flooded and a mess."

"Oh, okay," I said. I had wanted to talk to Clara, not all of my sisters. Clara had already met Bran and I knew she was the best listener. I didn't need advice from Lily and Lizzy, I just needed to talk a few things out.

Disappointed by the turn of events but seeing no way out of it, I got out of my truck and followed her inside.

"Hey Ruby," Lizzy said, genuinely smiling and hugging me when I walked in.

To be honest, the change in my sister still creeped me out. Her story was common knowledge now. She had met her one true mate as a teenager and then pushed him away when she thought it was best for the Pack, but their bond had never severed. She'd lived an empty life like a walking zombie. When Cole came back into her life, the change was instantaneous and it had scared the shit out of me.

I didn't understand how powerful a true bond was, and I sure as hell wasn't going to deny mine and risk living like Elizabeth had. That was the number one reason I didn't stop to think or challenge Bran when we bonded. What was the point? I knew I was meant to be with him, but being with anyone, even as sexy and amazing as my true mate was, was proving more difficult than I expected.

"Ruby? Did you even hear a word I said?" Lizzy asked.

"Huh? What? Sorry. Did you say something?"

The girls shared a look, and I knew I had just completely zoned out on them.

"She asked how things are going," Clara said sweetly. She always was the nicest of us all.

Before I could even open my mouth, Lily burst through the door. "Sister time!" she hollered.

"Oh Lord, have you been drinking already?" Clara asked.

Lily held up a bottle of vodka and toasted us all. "To sisters! I love you girls so much."

"That bottle is half empty. Please tell me you didn't drink the entire thing yourself," Lizzy said, though we all suspected the answer already.

"Did you drive over here?" I asked.

"Nope, Sydney drove me," she said as she tugged on something outside my view, and suddenly Sydney appeared.

I assumed things would have been awkward with the two. Then again, maybe that was why Lily was drunk. Sydney had been Thomas's longtime girlfriend. They had even been declared acceptable compatible mates by the Pack Council, and everyone thought Syd would be our next Pack Mother. That was until Lily visited from Westin Pack with my youngest sister, Madelyn. Lily and Maddie had been best friends since they were little girls.

Since Thomas and Lily are true mates, Sydney had bailed out gracefully and seemed truly happy for them. She had friended Lily and at times the two were inseparable—like now.

"Hey, guys. Sorry for the intrusion. I tried to tell her it was a bad idea to come over, but after Lizzy called, she insisted," Syd said.

"Shelby didn't want to come and Peyton's working," Lily announced as she plopped down on the couch. I chose the chair on the far side of the room. Nothing good ever came from Lily getting drunk. In fact, the last time she truly got this wasted, I believe she puked in Thomas's closet.

"I should go. Is she okay here or should I take her home?" Syd asked.

"Stay," I said, surprising everyone, but I knew if she stayed the heat would come off me some, because the second she left they were going to start questioning me about Bran.

The room got uncomfortably quiet for a minute as the girls settled into seats. Sydney chose to sit next to Lily, still looking like she was ready to bolt.

"Bran was teaching me and Thomas a drinking game before they took off for dinner. Apparently I sucked at the game, but it was so fun," Lily announced.

"Who's Bran?' Lizzy asked.

I shot her a look like she had two heads.

"Ruby's mate," Clara said, obviously filling her in.

"What?" she shrieked. "Ruby, you found your true mate?"

I nodded, still confused.

"Why am I just now hearing about this?"

I shrugged. "How the hell should I know? I assumed you'd already heard the rumors."

"I just got back into town today," she pointed out.

"Well, you were hanging out with Clara, so I figured she'd already told you," I said logically.

"I can't believe you didn't tell me. You could have called or something," Lizzy whined, looking genuinely upset.

"Psst, she was too busy with Bran. They hadn't even left her apartment before today," Lily informed her, causing my cheeks to heat.

"It's all anyone's talking about in town," Sydney added before shooting me an apologetic look.

"Well, where did you meet him? Where's he from? Tell me everything," Lizzy demanded.

"He was squatting on our land, and he's from that Indiana Pack we thought the Bulgarians wiped out," Lily filled her in.

I rolled my eyes. "That's not how we met, and I don't care what Pack he's from. I'm certainly glad the Bulgarians didn't kill him," I said with a snort.

"So how did you meet?" Clara asked.

"Cochise ran off, so I took Cinnamon out to look for him. I stumbled across Bran out there in the fields. He was holed up in one of the small groves. He said he got into an altercation with a couple Larkens and was pushed onto Collier land. Before that, some shifters in Boise had told him he could find work here," I told them.

"And you just knew? Like instantly, the way they say it happens?" Sydney asked in amazement.

All four of us nodded at her.

"There's never really any doubt," Clara said. "When you meet your true mate, Syd, you'll just know."

She sighed and looked a little starry-eyed. "Someday," she whispered.

"So what did you do? I mean, yeah, he was your mate, so your emotions were probably charged, but he was also a foreigner squatting on our land," Lizzy reminded me.

I shrugged. "He was my mate, Lizzy. What more is there to tell?"

"Are you going to bond with him?" she asked.

Suddenly it wasn't just my face on fire. The heat started to spread down my neck, highlighting my bond mark like a flashing neon sign.

I didn't say a word, but both Lily and Clara nodded, grinning as Lizzy processed what they were telling her.

"You already bonded with him?" she shrieked.

I shrugged, trying to play it off like it really wasn't that big a deal. "He's my true mate."

"It wasn't really clear to me when exactly that happened, though. I mean, you met him and you brought him back to your apartment. You were basically MIA for most of four days. How long did you wait?" Lily asked.

"They were already bonded when Gage and I met him for the first time. I'm pretty sure that was the day they met. I don't think they waited at all," Clara said.

Sydney bit her lip like she really wanted to say something but was fighting to keep it to herself.

"Fine! You really want to know?" I asked. They all nodded yes. "We didn't wait. Not one second. I stumbled across him in the woods a few miles from the barn. We knew instantly we were true mates, so we sealed the bond. Why fight it? I've seen what happens when you do, from you and you," I said, pointing to Lily and Lizzy. "And, I heard what happened with you," I told Clara. "I was not going through all that nonsense."

They burst out laughing.

"So, you just what, said, 'Hi, I'm Ruby, your mate,' and then jumped him right there and bonded with him?" Lily asked.

"That's about how it happened," I mumbled under my breath, crossing my arms over my chest.

They all got quiet.

"Holy shit, that really happened?" Sydney asked.

"Did you even know his name?" Lizzy asked, clearly in shock.

I rolled my eyes. "Of course I got his name first."

For some reason that made us all laugh this time.

"Wow, that's crazy, Ruby," Clara said. "I mean, I didn't know Gage for long when we sealed our bond, but at least I knew enough to understand what I was getting myself into."

I shrugged. "I don't think it would have changed things any, and probably for the best so we just dove right in."

"Because now it's been a few days, the sex has been amazing, but his little quirks are showing and driving you nuts, right?" Lily said.

"How long has it been?" Lizzy asked.

"Like four days or something like that," Lily informed her. "And they've barely come up for air before today."

"Oh yeah, he's driving you nuts," Lizzy said.

"Is it that obvious?" I blurted out. "I mean, seriously, he leaves his clothes on the floor next to the hamper. Next to it! It takes two extra seconds to lift the lid and actually put them inside. And he squeezes the toothpaste from the middle so it's all lumpy."

Clara giggled. "It's really not that you're obvious, it's just that we've been there and it's normal. Living with someone is hard, period."

"It downright sucks at times," Lizzy said.

"What? But you and Cole are so happy together."

My sister rolled her eyes. "I love Cole more than anything, but come on, the man is a health nut. Apparently you don't get that body without a lot of work and strict dieting. He keeps hiding my Pop-Tarts, telling me they aren't real food. He infuriates me!"

Lily snorted. "And does he fart in bed all the time? Because your brother sure does."

"Oh gross," Syd said. "I guess I dodged that bullet."

We all laughed.

"Gage is pretty great, most of the time, but he has a lot of past baggage to deal with and sometimes I just want to talk and he's off in his own head completely ignoring me. I try not to let it bother me, but sometimes I just want to slap him and tell him to snap out of it and pay attention to me," Clara confessed.

"So basically, true mates still have their flaws and that's normal. We what, just deal with it?" I asked.

"You'll complain, drive him just as batty, argue, and even occasionally fight," Lizzy said.

"But the makeup sex is worth it all," Lily admitted.

I looked at her in disgust. "Baby brother, remember? You can keep that shit to yourself."

Lily only shrugged. "I'm just telling it like it is."

"You guys make me glad I haven't found my true mate yet," Sydney said.

Lily hugged her. "You will, because you're amazing and wonderful and deserve to be the happiest of happy."

"That doesn't even make sense," I told her.

"Shhhh, just go with it," Lily said.

"How much did she drink?" Clara asked.

Sydney shrugged. "I don't know for sure. They kept refilling the shot glasses, but she really sucked at the game and drank more than they did and insisted she keep playing, swearing she was getting better. Thomas almost called it a night, but she convinced him she was fine, and I'd take care of her because it's ladies' night."

Lily's buzz must have been wearing off, because her eyes kept closing like she was going to fall asleep or pass out at any second.

"Maybe we should get her home," I suggested.

"I think you're right," Syd said.

"I'm fine, y'all. It's girl time. I love y'all so much."

"Uh-oh, it's never good when the 'I love yous' start coming out of her," Clara said.

"I'll help you get her to the car and follow you back, because I'm certain you're gonna need help getting her into the house," I said.

"You're leaving already?" Clara pouted.

"Yeah, I have to hunt up some dinner still and get home. I really appreciate you all telling me it's normal to get frustrated and want to strangle him sometimes," I admitted.

"I don't think we said it was okay to strangle him," Lizzy said, amused.

"Shhh, just go with it," Lily told her. "The makeup sex is worth it. I promise."

"Okay, she's going home now," I said.

Bran

Chapter 9

I almost felt guilty by the time I dropped Thomas off at his house. I had convinced him to drink vodka with me and play a few drinking games I knew I'd win easily. I had convinced myself I'd have to get him drunk for him to let me stay in the Pack, but as the evening wore on, I knew in my heart that wasn't the case.

Thomas Collier was genuinely a nice guy. He cared about his Pack and especially his family. He loved his sisters and only wanted to see them happy. He even commented that he'd never seen Ruby so happy as she was when he'd stopped by the apartment. I'd thought she'd been irritated and unhappy they were there, but as he'd told me several times, that was just Ruby's way, and he could tell she was happy.

He really believed in true mates and was head over heels in love with his mate. It didn't just show in his words, but in his actions, too. Bulgarians believed in mating for strength, but we were an isolated Pack that mostly kept to ourselves, so finding a true mate was rare. My father had always said that it had been sheer luck that he'd found his. I understood what he meant now. It felt like some divine force or just sheer damn luck that Ruby had stumbled across me literally in the middle of nowhere the way she had.

After seeing Thomas safely inside his house, I left the keys on his kitchen table and let myself out. He was stumbling down the hall towards the bedroom and I could hear Lily giggling and calling for him from the direction he was heading. I smiled and shook my head.

Lily had insisted on joining us, and it took her no time at all to lose enough to get drunk. She had a friend with her, and Thomas insisted they'd be fine. I'd also learned that her friend, Sydney, had almost been Thomas's mate. Not a true mate, but he'd obviously cared about the girl enough to go through compatibility testing with her and be approved for mating by the Council. That story had led into another round of the importance of true mates, and I'd learned more about Thomas Collier than I'd ever hoped to know. The most important thing, though, was that his biggest weakness was Lily.

I had left their house and stripped to shift to my wolf. I gathered my clothes in my mouth and ran back to the apartment. I looked around and, finding no one in the area, I shifted back and didn't bother getting dressed.

When I reached for the handle to the front door, I stilled. A shudder ran through my body. I hadn't seen Ruby since that morning. It was the longest I'd gone without her since the first moment I'd laid eyes on her. I felt her nearby and it excited my inner wolf. I could literally feel our bond had begun to grow and knowing Thomas's weakness now, I was terrified that Ruby would quickly become mine.

I took a deep breath and turned the knob. It was unlocked. I cursed under my breath. I knew it would be, but I hated that she refused to lock the door or show any concern for her own safety. I needed to remember to order new locks. I wouldn't be comfortable leaving her alone in this world until that happened.

She was asleep on the couch, snoring lightly and looking so beautiful. I stood there watching her, feeling myself grow hard with desire.

"Ruby," I said softly, but she didn't budge. I leaned down and shook her lightly, but still nothing. "Ruby, mate?" I tried again a little louder, shaking her a little harder.

She screamed, then shot up and started wailing her arms out in front of her like she was swatting a swarm of bees away, then she began kicking out, alternating legs and continued to spastically come after me. I wondered for a moment if she were having a seizure or something.

"Ruby," I said in a stern voice and she stilled. Opening her eyes fully, seeing me for the first time, she hauled off and punched me in the arm hard enough for it to sting.

"Don't scare me like that. You can't just sneak up on a lady while she's sleeping," Ruby yelled.

Confusion, then anger, then fear set in, and I pushed my wolf down as he sensed my emotions and needed to protect our mate.

"Sweetheart," I said, choosing an endearment I thought would soothe her and defuse the situation, but in truth it felt right to call her that. "What if I had been a stranger walking in to attack you. You never lock the doors. It could happen. Is that how you'd fight them off?"

"What?" she asked.

"You looked like a fish out of water having a seizure when you tried to attack me. Don't you know how to fight?"

She laughed at my description. "I can hit if I need to," she insisted.

I rubbed my bicep where she'd punched me. "I learned that, but one punch isn't fighting. Have you never learned to fight?"

"Why would I need to?" she said honestly.

"Well, I just scared you. It would have been in your right to fight back just now," I said.

Ruby frowned. "I thought I did."

I gave her a blank stare. "That was not fighting, Ruby. I don't have a clue what that was, but it definitely was not fighting."

She gave me a snort of indignation.

"Look, I just need to know you can take care of yourself if I'm not around. Just in case something bad happens."

"Bran, this is Collier. We're in the Middle-of-Nowhere, Wyoming. What bad stuff do you really think is going to happen?"

I shrugged. "I don't know. You don't know. That's why you train and learn to be prepared for anything."

She didn't look like she was buying it and crossed her arms over her chest in defiance. I tried to ignore them as they pushed up her breasts, inviting me to close the gap to claim my mate and forget all about this conversation.

"Well?" she asked. "What sort of danger do you foresee happening in Collier?"

I scrunched up my brow. "When the Bulgarians attacked Westin Pack, do you think they had time to stop and learn to fight? No. If they hadn't already been prepared who knows what would have happened in that battle."

"But we're not at war with anyone," she tried to point out logically.

"They weren't either, that's my point. By the time something does arise it's too late to start training. You have to prepare in advance." I could tell she wasn't entirely sold. "Okay, how about something closer to home, more realistic. What if it hadn't been me who walked in and instead someone wanted to force himself on you? You were asleep and vulnerable, Ruby. I could have had my way with you before you even knew what was happening."

She shuddered. "My sister Madelyn was gang raped," she said softly.

"I'm sorry. I didn't know that. I'm not trying to terrify you, I just want to keep you safe, even when I'm not around to do that for you," I said honestly. I knew there would be a day much too soon when I would no longer be here to protect her. Every ounce of my being needed to know she was going to be okay after I was gone.

"It's not really something we talk a lot about. It happened a long time ago," she said.

"Okay, different scenario then. When I came into the area, I had a skirmish with some Larken wolves who pushed me into Collier territory. What if that were you? You were riding alone out there on the range when you found me, sweetheart. What if it hadn't been me? What if it had been those Larken wolves you stumbled across out there all alone? What would you have done then?"

She shuddered again. "That happened to Lizzy once. She's really fast and was able to outrun them until help came. I would have had Cinnamon and they wouldn't have gotten me on horseback," she said confidently.

I sighed. "You weren't on horseback, Ruby. You were alone on foot, in that wooded patch."

Her eyes dilated and I saw that she finally understood what I was saying.

"But . . ." she hesitated. I knew she was thinking through various scenarios and the frown that spread across her beautiful face told me she wasn't winning even her imaginary situations. Her shoulders sagged in defeat. "Will you teach me to fight, Bran? Like real, proper fighting, then?"

I bit back a victorious grin and kept a solemn face when I nodded. "We'll start tomorrow right after work. I'll set up a full training schedule immediately. Hand-to-hand, weapons, and wolf."

She looked a little surprised at how quickly I'd agreed. She didn't seem to realize, that was the entire point of the conversation, and what I'd wanted all along.

It had been a long day. I scooped Ruby up into my arms as she squealed and leaned in to kissed me. I carried my sexy mate to our bed and made love to her. It was not the wild and crazy sex we often shared; this was different, more intimate, and afterwards as I lay awake with her safely snuggled against me sleeping soundly, I reflected on my biggest fears. Ruby was easy to love and I could already see a long, happy life with her in my arms, but that couldn't be, and I couldn't tell her why.

I had easily noticed the little things that irked my mate and vowed to keep doing them and find others that equally pissed her off. I might be falling in love with Ruby, but I couldn't stomach her truly falling for me, too. Not when I knew the heartache I would inevitably cause her.

Eventually I did fall asleep and when I awoke the next morning, Ruby was already up. I heard her rustling around in the kitchen. I jumped out of bed and found the clothes I'd worn yesterday on the chair in the living room.. I took them back to our bedroom, sure to leave them in a pile on the floor next to the hamper. I quickly brushed my teeth, and this time not only did I squeeze the toothpaste from the middle, which secretly drove me just as nuts, but I grimaced as I left the cap off and dribbled a glob down in the sink before jumping in the shower.

Halfway through my shower Ruby came in to finish getting ready. Even over the pounding water I heard her curse and growl loudly. I grinned, fighting hard not to laugh out loud.

Despite how infuriated she was with me over the little things, when I was out of the shower, dressed and ready to start the day, she still had breakfast waiting for me on the table. It was a small gesture, but it meant more to me than I could possibly say.

I pulled her close to me and marveled at how the tension she was carrying melted away at my touch. I kissed her until she sighed and pressed her body fully against me.

Pulling back, I smiled at the dazed look in her eyes. "Thank you for making breakfast. Have a great day at work."

She nodded, then blushed. "We didn't talk about what Thomas said. Did he find you a job?"

I nodded. "I start this morning. I'll be working out on the range with Wyatt today."

"Oh, good. Wyatt's great. He's very close friends with Thomas and will report anything you do or say back to him."

I laughed. "After enough drinks in him, Thomas told me as much last night."

She shook her head. "Someday you're going to have to teach me that drinking game. Lily was completely sloshed when she showed up at Clara's."

She gave me another quick kiss, wished me a good first day, and disappeared. I checked the time, scarfed down the breakfast, and headed out the door myself. I beat Wyatt to our meeting place by five minutes.

A quick assessment of the guy told me he was cut from the same cloth as Thomas, just a genuinely good guy. It set my nerves on edge. I had prepared for a lot of circumstances before agreeing to this assignment but falling in love with a sassy redhead and liking the men I met along the way wasn't something I had foreseen, or even considered as a possibility. In some ways, I supposed it helped the situation, but there was also a twinge of guilt that set in every time I thought about it and what it would do to Ruby.

That woman was a spitfire. She could talk some smack, but she couldn't fight worth a shit. Before I proceeded with my mission, I needed to know she was capable of handling whatever backlash she got from my actions, and things were moving at a much faster rate than I had anticipated. There was no time to waste.

The work day was easy, peaceful. Wyatt was just out checking conditions on the range. That basically meant we spent the day riding horses out in the open fields. He explained that sometimes an animal would stray off and we would be responsible for finding it. Certain times of year cattle runs were necessary, or roundups to bring them back in, but early spring with no threat of snow in the forecast made for pleasant rides and downtime.

The guys rotated jobs so no one was ever stuck doing the same thing day in and day out. The rotation usually came in two-week intervals and this was the easiest, when everything was going right. When things weren't, it could be a rough one, he had explained.

I loved being outdoors and the wide-open fields, the rolling hills, the river, even the small patches of woods felt like a little slice of heaven on Earth and I was happy. Happy wasn't something I'd been in a very long time. The peaceful feeling of contentment with my new life scared me because I knew the blood oath I'd taken would never allow any of this to be real or permanent.

I tried not to let that thought depress me and spent the rest of the morning chatting with Wyatt as we rode along. I learned his mate owned the diner we had gotten takeout from on my first night in town. He also told me about the Six Pack and growing up with Thomas. Dammit if I didn't like the guy even more by the time we headed in for lunch.

Lunch was served in a chow hall. There were two shifts and just about everyone that worked the ranch—farm, range, animals, or dairy—came to the chow hall for lunch.

When we walked in, I subconsciously began searching the room until my eyes rested on the curly haired redhead surrounded by a table full of men. My wolf growled in my head when she threw back her head and laughed at something one of them said.

"Come on," Wyatt said, nudging me with his arm after we'd made it through the food line with our trays. I followed him, but never took my eyes off Ruby.

As we approached her table, I saw her still in awareness and turn to look around for me. That small motion made my wolf instantly calm.

"Move down and give the girl some space, Austin," Wyatt said. "She's a taken woman now," he casually announced to them all, making Ruby blush.

I didn't hesitate to take the abandoned seat next to her. She awkwardly hit her elbow against my arm. "Hey, how's it going today?"

"Good. Wyatt's a great teacher," I said.

Ruby didn't have to tell me that it had not always been easy for her being a lady in the middle of a male-dominated world. Looking around, there were only three other females in the room. She had been at ease and just one of the guys when we'd walked in, and her unease and tension now told me she didn't know what to do or say with me there.

I tried to relax my wolf some more by pressing my leg against hers. It seemed to work, and I purposefully kept the conversation to business only, not even looking her way, but sneaking little ways to let her know I was well aware of my mate.

I met the rest of the Six Pack Wyatt had told me about. We shared a few stories, laughed, and kept things amicable. Ruby relaxed and joined back in as if I were just another one of the guys. She particularly liked to rib Austin, who always seemed to be asking for it anyway.

Wyatt announced we had to leave, and I begrudgingly got up to follow. I didn't care about the other guys, though I was having a good time with them. I was anxious leaving my mate with them again. I tried to fight down that aggressive surge to protect her. I knew it wouldn't be wanted in this situation.

"Back to work, you guys," Ruby said as she got up to leave and follow us out. As soon as we were outside, she took my hand and gave me a quick kiss on my cheek. "Thank you," she said, and I knew she genuinely meant it.

I didn't know how to respond to that, so I just nodded. She gave my hand a final squeeze and headed off for the dairy barn as Wyatt and I turned to walk back to the stables where we'd left our horses.

"It hasn't always been easy for Ruby around here. She works harder than any of us, mostly just trying to prove the point she's just as good as any man. Truth is we all know she's far better than any of us. You did good in there. I could sense your wolf was struggling. Even bonded, it's never easy to see your mate surrounded by a bunch of other males, especially unbonded ones."

"Does it ever get easier?" I asked him.

"Nah," he assured me with a smile. "I still want to rip the throats out of every single male that goes up in the diner and flirts with my woman. Our wolves have a natural need to protect what's ours at all costs, but thankfully our human sides know when to roll it back and when to step in. Not reacting today was the right thing for Ruby."

"Thanks, Wyatt. I suspected as much, but it's nice to hear."

The rest of the day passed quickly and soon I was saying goodbye and heading for home.

When I walked in the house smelled wonderful of roast. "Honey, I'm home," I teased as I found her in the kitchen.

She turned and wrapped her arms around my neck and kissed my lips. It was the perfect ending to a good day.

"Dinner will be ready in about two hours. I just put it in."

"Wow, it smells great already," I said.

She laughed. "That's your wolfie senses speaking. I promise, that roast is still raw."

"Well, how about you go and change into workout clothes and we'll get started on your training then?"

"You were serious about that?"

I gave her a look that said I was not only serious but there was no room for negotiation.

"Fine. I'll go change," she said before heading off to the bedroom.

I started to follow her, then thought better of it. If I went into that bedroom with her, we wouldn't come back out until the roast was burning. When I heard the bathroom door close, I ran in and changed quickly. I was already in the living room moving the furniture out of the way when she came back out.

Ruby frowned. "We're training in here?"

"For today. I want to assess where you're at so I can proceed from there. Have you at least gone through mating challenge training?" I prayed she said yes knowing she could be challenged at any time. Thomas should be making a Pack announcement soon and that too would leave her vulnerable.

"Sure I did. As a teenager we were all expected to train for challenges."

I scuffed my face with my hands. "As a teen. Great. How much do you actually remember?"

She shrugged. "I was okay. I'm also the third daughter. Seriously, who would want to challenge me?"

"Ruby, you're the daughter of an Alpha, and now that we're mated, anyone could issue a challenge against you. I need you to take this seriously."

She gave me a comical look. "No, they can't."

"What? Of course they can. For the next four months you are vulnerable to challenges. Thomas will be making a Pack announcement any day now about our mating."

"That's archaic, Bran. There's a push back to the Grand Council about challenges regarding true mates. We're true mates. Thomas petitioned them to change the rules, along with several other Packs. Until the Grand Council formally addresses their appeal, no announcement, no accepted challenges for true mates. Period. If that's what this is all about, then you can stop worrying. I'm safe."

"I've never heard of such a thing," I said aloud, but more to myself.

"Ask Thomas about it if you don't believe me."

"You're my mate, I will always believe you above all else, but that changes nothing. I will rest more comfortably when I know you can protect yourself from any situation, so we train."

For the next hour I put her through a grueling workout to test her endurance, her strength, and her weaknesses. She was in excellent shape and her motor skills were solid, but she was easily distracted, and her combat movements were slow. I needed her to commit them to muscle memory. Using a Japanese karate technique, I gave her a pattern of movements to practice, similar to a kata but representing those motions I needed her to memorize.

We went over the movements slowly as I demonstrated the blocks, strikes, and even a roundhouse kick. She duplicated my motions as we repeated the pattern over and over until at last Ruby collapsed onto the couch, flushed and sweaty and begging for a break.

I looked at the time and knew our dinner would be ready soon.

"That's enough for today. You can go shower and I'll listen for the buzzer on the oven," I told her.

As she left with a groan, I searched around until I found a piece of paper and a pen. I quickly jotted down notes of what I'd had her do, how she'd responded, what I'd assessed, and the kata I had put together for her to practice.

She was back just as the oven sounded, but looking exhausted, so I tended to the remainder of our meal and served her. There was something very satisfying about meeting my mate's needs in this way.

When dinner was done, I shooed her away and cleaned up. After dishes were done, I showered, not even bothering to put on the pajamas I had borrowed from Gage. I knew my first paycheck would come the next week and I planned to take whatever money I made and invest in new clothes so I could return the loaned ones.

Ruby watched me as I walked towards the bed and she groaned, sounding completely miserable. "Every muscle in my body is already aching," she whined.

I knew she thought I expected sex. I climbed into my side of the bed and pulled the covers over me, then I reached out to her. "I only wish to hold my mate tonight," I assured her.

She turned wondrous eyes my way like she was trying to assess if I was being serious. I almost chuckled. True, we'd gone at it like rabbits for days and I doubted I would ever get enough of her, but there was more to being mated than just the sex.

"I can go an entire day without sex, you know," I said with a laugh. "Come here." I pulled her to me and she sighed contentedly as she rested her head on my chest. I kissed the top of her curls. "Sweet dreams."

Ruby

Chapter 10

I got up the next morning feeling a little sore. It had been the best sleep I'd had in ages though, and I was running a little behind. Bran was already up and making breakfast. He had been so attentive after my training the night before and I felt spoiled. *I can definitely get used to this,* I thought.

I noticed immediately there were no clothes on the floor next to the hamper. I brushed away that little voice that reminded me it was probably because he hadn't bothered to put on pajamas the night before and didn't have any clothes to leave on the floor.

Bran was at the stove cooking bacon. There was a plate full of eggs on the counter and a heaping pile of sausage and ham, too. The smells made my stomach rumble, but the sight of my gorgeous mate in the kitchen made my mouth water.

I wrapped my arms around his waist from behind. "Good morning."

I could hear the smile in his voice when he said, "Good morning to you, too. Grab some breakfast before you go. I'm almost done here.

I let him go, to get a plate and help myself. He tossed on a couple of extra pieces of bacon on top, then turned off the stove and filled his own plate full.

We ate in comfortable silence, then I gave him a quick kiss before running out of the house. I was a few minutes late, which wasn't like me at all. Even knowing no one would care, it bothered me to be late.

"Ruby girl, I was just about to come and find you. Doc was by this morning to check on the animals and looks like Mellie is showing signs of labor. I knew you would want to be with her, so I went ahead and changed the schedule around some to free you up," Mr. Draper said.

"You really think today's the day?"

"It's looking promising, but could be tomorrow," he said excitedly.

I gave him a quick hug and kiss on the cheek. "Thank you for taking care of that. I really do appreciate it. Who's looking after the dairy?"

"Clay volunteered when he heard. He's floating this week anyway and said it was that or ride with Wyatt all day and listen to him ramble on about how awesome it is to be mated."

I laughed. "Bran's riding with him, so that could have been doubly as bad."

"I guess I dodged a bullet and made the right choice then," Clay said from behind me as he walked into the barn. "Go on, check on your new mama. I can handle things here."

"You're the best! Thanks, Clay," I said, meaning it. Clay was always the one I could count on. He was the first to step up and pitch in when times got tough, or something unexpected happened, like Mellie going into labor, or my mate showing up out of the blue. I knew he always had my back around the barn.

I left the two men talking and headed back to the nursery. I stopped to say hello to the young calves as I made my way back to Mellie.

"Good morning, Mellie," I said, and noticed the cow turn and try to waddle to me. I jumped the gate and met her halfway. I rubbed my hand over her fur and leaned down to kiss her nose.

We hadn't had the cattle for that long. It wasn't until a bad winter nearly wiped out our harvest and almost bankrupted the Pack that my father began expanding the ranch to include the animals. Before that we only really had horses. Now there were chickens, cows, pigs, goats, and even rabbits. Our newest additions were a small herd of bison. The cows were still my favorite.

It had taken a while for the animals to adjust. Our wolves spooked them easily at first, but over time we had all adjusted and while in human form, the animals seemed unaffected by our wolves. Many of them weren't even bothered in our fur anymore. We had all evolved and coexisted peacefully.

Mellie shook and I continued to soothe her, talking in a calm, low voice that I knew she liked. I spent most of the day there just like that. I saw the signs of her labor increase, but knew it would take some time before the new babies arrived.

Clay came in around lunchtime to check on me.

"Mr. Draper is coming by to sit with Mellie so you can get yourself some lunch. Come on. He gave me explicit orders to escort you over and make sure you eat."

I smiled. That certainly sounded like something the old man would say.

"We should stay until he gets here," I said.

"Would you just listen for once," Mr. Draper said as he walked in. "Stop being stubborn and go with the boy."

"Fine," I said, begrudgingly. "But if anything changes . . ."

"I'll come find you myself," he said.

"Fine," I said again as I told Mellie goodbye, promising to be right back.

I followed Clay to the chow hall, and the moment I walked in I felt Bran's presence. I smiled, got a plate, and took my usual seat at the table where my mate was waiting.

"Everything okay?" he asked casually.

"Great. Mellie's in labor. I may not make it home tonight if she doesn't deliver soon."

"That's the mama cow, right?"

I smiled and nodded, pleased that he had listened and knew who I was talking about.

"I'll come by and check on you when I get home this afternoon. I can keep you company on baby watch if you'd like," he offered.

He had been so sweet, finishing up dinner last night, not being pushy or demanding when I was sore from his training, and making breakfast this morning. I could even overlook the blob of toothpaste he'd left in the sink and the toilet lid that was up and almost caused me to fall in when I got up to pee in the middle of the night. Bran was simply perfect, and my heart swelled with happiness.

"I'd like that," I finally managed to say, trying not to show how choked up his offer was making me.

Austin and Emmett shared a look, but since they refrained from commenting, I held back my need to kick them both under the table. Instead, they turned their attention to Bran and started asking him how things were going and how he liked working with Wyatt.

I stayed unusually quiet throughout lunch, as Bran took the spotlight. I was totally fine with that though and enjoyed a peaceful meal where I didn't feel like I had to be the center of attention the entire time.

When lunch was over, Wyatt told Bran it was time to go.

He squeezed my knee under the table, and I surprised us both by giving him a quick kiss on the lips before saying goodbye.

To their credit, Austin and Emmett kept their mouths shut until Bran and Wyatt had left the building. Before they could even finish their first thought, I kicked Austin hard under the table, stood up, grabbed my plate and stormed off.

I had worked hard to earn my place amongst the men. I had taken more shit than any of them over the years and I deserved the position of authority I was now in. That wasn't something that was just handed to me as an Alpha's kid. I'd made it a point never to show weakness or femininity around the ranch. Sure, I had messed around with a few of them over the years, but always after hours with a strict policy that it never bled over to the work day. So why did I just kiss Bran in front of all of them?

I knew the answer—because he was my mate. It was really that simple. He was different. He was the exception. I wasn't going to sit there and hear Austin and Emmett belittle that or tease me about it, but it was a truth I needed to deal with. Bran and I were working together, maybe not in the same position, and I was glad Thomas hadn't assigned him to work in the dairy under me, but the ranch was one big family, and my mate was a part of that now.

By the time I got back to Mellie, I had come to terms with it all. It was going to be fine. Plus, Bran was teaching me to fight and if anyone had crap to say about it, I'd just kick his ass. I was grinning evilly when Mr. Draper looked up and shook his head.

"Whatever you're thinking can't be good. I know that look too well."

I laughed. "It's fine."

Clay wandered in. "What's fine?"

Mr. Draper shrugged. "Your guess is as good as mine. I'm going to leave you two and go check on my horses now."

"Thanks for all your help today," I told him.

"So what's fine?"

"Everything," I told him. "I'm guessing you saw me kiss Bran at lunch."

"He's your mate, isn't he? There's nothing wrong with that, Ruby," he said.

"I know. It's just . . ."

"You've worked hard at being a badass and trying to fit in with the boys all these years. I know, Ruby. But truth is, you've always stood out and no one would ever truly consider you one of the guys." He held up his hand when I started to protest. "I'm not saying we don't see you as an equal. You've more than earned that respect around here, but as one of the guys? Never. Though everyone pretends so for your benefit, until you turn around and they all start checking out your ass."

"Clay," I growled, smacking him on the arm.

He gave me a sly grin. "What? You know you have a great ass."

Clay stayed with me for a while then excused himself to check on the shift change with the dairy cows. Mellie wasn't progressing quickly, and I found myself dozing off on a bale of hay as I watched her.

Bran shook me awake some time later.

"Hey," I said in a groggy voice.

"Hey yourself. Are you sure you don't want to go up and take a real nap? I can stay with the cow if you're worried," he offered.

"I'm fine," I insisted. "Plus, I just had a nap. Are you done with work already?"

I nodded. "Yeah, and Wyatt's bringing dinner over in a couple hours after the rush at the diner. He warned me we could be pulling an all-nighter, so I didn't think you'd mind a late dinner."

"No, that's perfect. Thank you." I kissed him. "You're perfect," I mumbled against his lips before deepening the kiss.

A throat clearing interrupted us. I looked up with a scowl.

"Oh, hey, doc. Are you coming to check on Mellie?" I asked, surprised to see him. Doc usually tended to the shifters, not the animals. We had a vet on call for that.

"Yes, Davidson and I have been alternating weeks for on call to give him a break until the two new vets are up and ready to work on their own."

I frowned. "Clara's home. Should I call her in to assist?"

Doc laughed. "Ruby, I assure you, I'm perfectly capable of delivering the calf. It really isn't that much different than any human or shifter delivery," he pointed out.

"Calves," I reminded him. "Mellie's carrying two."

"Oh dear, he didn't mention that in his report. That could cause some complications."

"I know. We should call him back in. I don't care if he's on call or not. And maybe Clara too."

"Clara's been hanging out around the clinic, getting bored between assignments. I think she'd be happy to assist tonight if it will make you feel better. Remember, we're still just on baby watch, she's not in active labor yet."

"No, but it can go quickly when the time comes," I told him.

I had sat up with enough of my girls and seen enough deliveries to know what to expect, even with the added concern of twins. In truth I could probably deliver the babies myself, but I didn't mention that. I was no expert and I wouldn't dare put one of my girls at risk trying to pretend I was.

I picked up my cell and dialed Clara.

"Hello?"

"Hey Clara. Do you have plans tonight?"

"No, not really. Gage and I were just settling in for a movie. Why?"

"Mellie's in labor and could deliver tonight," I told her.

"Mellie? That name doesn't ring a bell. Do I know her?"

"One of my cows, Clara. Keep up," I said.

"Oh, one of your girls is expected to deliver tonight. I got it now. Do you want me to come and keep you company, like we did as kids? Barnyard slumber party? I could call the girls and get them over too, just like old times."

I laughed at the memories.

"Well, Bran is staying with me, and Doc's here."

"Doc? Where's Davidson?"

"He's off tonight and Doc's on call for him. I'm a little nervous," I admitted.

Clara laughed. "Sweetie, you always get nervous when one of your girls is about to deliver. Just imagine how much worse you'll be when one of us gets pregnant."

"I'm not that bad," I said, rolling my eyes even knowing she couldn't see me. "It's just that Mellie's expecting twins."

Clara paused for only a moment. "I'm on my way. You said Bran's there? Mind if I bring Gage, too?"

"Now that sounds like a modern-day barnyard slumber party to me."

I hung up the phone and let Doc know that Clara was coming to stay the night.

"Do you want some sister time then? Should I go upstairs?" Bran asked.

"No, Gage is tagging along too. It'll be fun," I assured him.

Bran

Chapter 11

I really didn't think hanging out with her sister and mate in a barn, watching a cow give birth, was my idea of fun, but I knew I wasn't going anywhere else, either.

Half an hour later Clara and Gage strolled in, with Elizabeth and Cole Anderson. My heart stilled for a moment, thinking they were on to me. Cole Anderson was a Westin Pack Beta. I knew he and his mate split their time between Westin and Collier Packs, but my resources told me they weren't due back in Collier for another two months.

"Hey, you guys. I didn't know you were coming too. Are you staying?" Ruby asked as she rose to hug her sisters.

I stood too and shook Gage's hand and accepted the hug Clara offered. I had only met them once, briefly, on the night I'd arrived.

"Bran, this is my oldest sister Lizzy, and her mate, Cole. Guys, this is my mate, Bran," Ruby said as she introduced us.

"Hey, it's nice to meet you both," I said cordially, trying to slow my racing heart.

Wolf shifters had fantastic hearing and that meant that we could generally tell when someone was lying or nervous by the cadence of their heart. It had saved my hide numerous times, and while most shifters gave little thought to something like that, Cole Anderson was the kind of man to take notice.

"Is the house still flooded?" Ruby asked. I looked at her in confusion. "Oh, yeah, you were with Thomas when we were talking about that the other night. Lizzy and Cole got called home, only to find their place flooded."

"Busted pipe," Cole said with gritted teeth. "It's been a bitch to clean up, but at least Gage and I found the break and were able to repair it."

"So no more water pouring in, but we still have plenty that pooled all over the house to deal with, and the flooring to rip up and replace, and who knows what else," Lizzy added.

Cole wrapped an arm around his mate and pulled her close to his side. He affectionately kissed the top of her head and I knew he was trying to reassure her that everything was going to be okay.

"Ignore them," Clara said. "Their bond is fully sealed, and they often zone out and forget to include anyone else in the room as they speak telepathically to each other."

I was confused. I thought they had only just bonded within the last year. A sealed bond usually took decades to achieve.

"I know what you're thinking, but it's true," Ruby said. "Their bond started as they were just kids really, and despite years of separation I guess it just kept growing. When they finally mated last year, their bond fully sealed almost immediately."

Cole grinned happily down at his mate. He looked content, where I had always heard he was a dark and ominous man.

"I didn't know something like that was possible," I said.

"Neither did we until it happened to us," Cole said. "But after the years of hell we both went through with our bond in limbo, it was the greatest gift ever."

I looked at Ruby and saw the emotions playing across her face. She had told me she bonded with me so quickly because she'd seen firsthand what an unresolved bond did to a person and she would never live that way. I suspected that person was Lizzy.

My hand found its way to her waist on its own accord and I tugged her closer to me, sensing she needed the contact.

"So we brought blankets and snacks," Gage said, changing the subject quickly. "Where do you want us to set up?"

Ruby stepped from my grasp and showed them around and told them where to put their things. I stood back and watched, then remembered we had dinner coming in about an hour.

"Hey, have you guys had dinner already? Wyatt's bringing Ruby and me over something in a little while from the diner. Anyone need anything?" I asked.

"We've been staying at Clara and Gage's," Lizzy said. "We were finishing up dinner when Ruby called, but thanks for the offer."

I nodded. Everyone in Collier seemed sincerely nice. They cared about each other and took the time to say as much. It didn't even feel like the same world I'd grown up in. My father had led our Pack like a commander led his battalion. We all had each other's backs, but there were no genuine feelings towards one another. The simple gestures like a little "thank you for thinking of me even though I don't need what you're offering," or the handshake Wyatt greeted me with every morning at work, those things made this place stand out above anywhere I'd ever been before. They weren't demanded or required, they were real emotions, and they were screwing with my head.

It had barely been a week since I'd arrived in Collier territory and I could feel the place changing me. I couldn't run away and just go back home. My Alpha would never accept that. The blood oath would kick in and force my actions back towards the goal of killing Elena the witch anyway. I was stuck with no way out of that. It was the true reason my Alpha had insisted on the oath. Maybe he already understood the harder things I'd face here, like love and respect, concepts only before that I couldn't possibly have prepared myself to face. I would never know for certain because my path was already written.

For the first time, that thought terrified me. Regardless of whether my plans to kill the witch were successful or not, I knew I wouldn't survive them. If I killed her, they would hunt me down and kill me anyway. If I didn't, I would die trying. Either way I had already signed my death certificate and there was no going back from it.

"Are you okay?" Ruby asked, probably sensing my sullenness.

I looked over at my beautiful mate, grateful for the short time I'd already had with her and vowed again to make the most of every second we were given together.

I smiled at her in reassurance. "I'm fine. How's our mama doing?"

Ruby beamed at my question and launched into the latest update. She didn't stop talking about her until Wyatt showed up with dinner. Not wanting to eat in front of the others, we snuck upstairs to our apartment and ate our meal in peace.

I cleaned up behind her as Ruby sat watching.

"You're too good to me, do you know that?"

In truth, I was plagued by guilt over the situation I'd put her in. Unable to express that to her, I focused instead on how much I had already grown to care for her, and I wanted to show her with actions instead of words.

I pulled her to stand from where she sat at our small kitchen table and I wrapped my arms around her. I heard her sharp intake of breath as I crushed my lips to hers. They parted easily for me as my tongue delved into her mouth, exploring and tasting.

She pressed her body tightly against mine and my physical response left no question for how much I wanted her. She moaned softly against my lips and I pulled her impossibly closer to me. I could feel her nipples harden against my chest, even through our clothing.

As my hand moved lower to the hem of her shirt, the phone rang.

With a frustrated growl, she slowly pulled back and answered it. Her flushed cheeks lit up in a different light.

"She's progressing quickly. Clara doesn't think it will be long before the first babe makes its appearance," she told me excitedly.

I took her hand and resolutely led us to the door. I knew how important this was and my physical needs would wait. What mattered more was what Ruby needed and I knew she didn't want to miss the birth of the calves. It was obvious just how important the animals around the farm were to her.

I tried to discreetly adjust myself and will down the hard-on I was sporting after that kiss. Ruby giggled and I knew she was watching me.

"I'm sorry," she whispered.

I shook my head. "I have you for the rest of my life. Those babies aren't going to wait."

It was true, even though I knew my life would end far too soon.

There was already excitement growing around the barn when we got back. Lizzy shot us a knowing look and I knew she thought we'd disappeared to feast on each other and not our dinner. Oh, how I'd wished that had been true. I was still walking around in an uncomfortable state.

"Sorry," Gage said, taking notice of my situation. "I told her to hold off until it was time, but she didn't want Ruby getting pissed if she missed the first birth."

"It's okay. This is really important to my mate. It was the right call," I assured him.

The girls all huddled around the laboring animal, tending to her needs while Gage and I hung back and watched. Cole Anderson soon joined us.

"Is it finally dry enough to start pulling up flooring tomorrow?" Gage asked him.

"Hell if I know. I'll check it in the morning. I hope so. I hadn't planned on returning here till mid-spring and I have things pressing back home. We couldn't just ignore the situation though."

"I've started working during the day, but we usually finish up mid-afternoon if you need an extra hand," I surprised myself by volunteering.

"Hey, that would be great, really. I could use all the help I can get. Thomas and a few of his friends will be pitching in this weekend, too. If you're available then, that would be awesome," Cole said.

"Sure. I don't think we have anything planned for the weekend," I said, thinking of all the ways I really wanted to spend the weekend, alone and naked with Ruby under me. I bit back a groan at the vivid images floating through my mind.

Cole laughed. "That is, if you're ready to leave your apartment. How long have you and Ruby been bonded?"

I sighed. "Almost a week."

"And she's already back to work?"

"They both are," Gage filled him in.

Cole shook his head. "How long did you go through mating before sealing the bond?"

I grinned. "Long enough to catch her name first. Maybe ten minutes."

Gage laughed out loud and Cole scowled. "That's it?" he asked.

I shrugged. "Honestly, I think I have you to thank for that."

Cole's scowl deepened, lost in dark memories. I shivered to think of what he'd gone through. An unresolved bond was rarely spoken of, but I'd heard the nightmarish stories that came with such a thing.

"Well, that's a good thing, but how are you adjusting? I mean, the mating period may be a mess, but it allows time to get to know your mate, fall in love, and adjust to a myriad of raging hormones. That level of aggression does ease with bonding, but it never fully goes away."

I shrugged. "I guess I hadn't considered all that. It's not easy seeing her in the chow hall surrounded by a bunch of unmated males, but I've been able to keep it in check."

"Has she claimed you publicly yet?" Gage surprised me by asking.

"What do you mean?"

"You know, shown affection around those guys? Told them verbally that you're mated? Taken you out in public around town?"

"Um . . ." I thought through our week. "Yes, today after lunch, she kissed me when she got up to go back to work. Sort of, or at least I know the other guys are all aware she's off the market. And no, not yet. I'm waiting for my first paycheck to come in next week to venture into town and replace those clothes I borrowed from you."

"No rush on that, seriously. Clara likes to shop, and I have entirely too much as it is," Gage informed me.

"When she opens up and introduces you around some and you can basically let others in the area know she's yours, then your wolf will probably start to settle some. But overall, if you can even stand to walk into the chow hall with her sitting there surrounded by a bunch of males, then it sounds like you're already in a good place. My wolf still has territorial issues where Elizabeth's concerned," Cole confessed.

"After all you went through, that's not surprising though," Gage reminded him.

I kept my mouth shut. Something told me I really didn't want the gory details of what that had been like all those years.

Elizabeth came out to join us.

"How's it going in there?" Gage asked.

"False alarm, her labor has stalled. We've got blankets and munchies set up in there if you guys want to join us."

"Sure," I said, as we followed her back inside. It looked like the entire stable area where the cow was being kept had been transformed. There were colorful blankets strewn across stacks of haybales, and a mess of food scattered all around.

Ruby motioned for me to join her on one of the blankets as the other guys joined their mates, too. Doc excused himself with instructions to call if the cow showed any signs of advancing again, but said he wanted to go home and catch a few hours of sleep while things were stagnant.

"Looks like we're in for an all-nighter," Clara announced.

"Did anyone call Lily and Thomas and let them know?" Lizzy asked.

"No, why would we?" Ruby asked.

Her sister shrugged. "I don't know. I've been gone a while and I missed you guys. It would be nice to just hang out with everyone tonight."

Ruby rolled her eyes. "Should I call Peyton and Shelby, too?"

"Yes!" Clara and Lizzy said excitedly.

I hadn't really met Ruby's family yet and it felt like I was about to be tossed into the fire.

Within an hour the others all showed up. Thomas shook my hand and officially welcomed me to the family—not his Pack, but his family. In some odd way that felt even more important to me.

Peyton was a little on the shy side and quieter than the others. Shelby immediately hugged me and thanked me for putting up with her sister. I had to laugh at the daggers Ruby shot her way.

Throughout the night I got to really know each of the Collier kids. They razzed each other constantly and shared embarrassing stories, especially about Ruby, who seemed to hold the spotlight for the night, but the overall love they shared was hard to ignore.

I had never once felt love or a need to share anything with my brothers. The entire concept was foreign to me, but it was nice and comforting.

As a new day arrived, people started getting tired. A few began to doze off, and smaller groups formed for quiet chats. Ruby stayed by my side and I could tell she was fighting off sleep when her head began to bob.

"Hey, come on," I said, rising and taking her hand to pull her up with me.

We walked out into the next room. It was quiet and there was plenty of space.

"What are we doing?" Ruby asked, rubbing sleep from her eyes.

"I know you're trying to stay awake, so I thought maybe if we got your blood pumping you'd at least get through the next few hours."

She lowered her voice and gave me a stern looking. "Bran, all my siblings are in the next room. I'm not . . ."

I chuckled but kissed her quickly before she could finish her statement and change my mind to head in that direction.

"That's not what I was thinking, but our apartment is just upstairs if you want that sort of break," I said with a smirk. "What I was going to suggest is we walk through the motions you learned yesterday and maybe do a little sparring."

Her forehead crinkled and she looked a little confused before I saw the resolve set in.

"Fine, but go easy on me, my muscles are already beginning to rebel and they say day two after a new workout is always the worst."

"There's some truth to that, but day three, four, and so on will be a lot easier if you don't stop, and actually train your muscles properly."

She got into position next to me without a fuss, and side by side we walked through the motions, slowly at first, then picking up speed with each round.

Peyton wandered out at some point and started watching us.

"What are you doing?" she asked in between sets.

"Bran thinks I fight like a girl and need to be able to fend for myself, so he's teaching me self-defense," Ruby said.

"Can I do it, too?" Peyton asked. "I've been practicing a little on my own using some YouTube videos, but it would be nice to have a partner to actually practice with."

"Pey, is everything okay?" Ruby asked sounding very concerned.

"It's fine, just something that's been weighing on me. I mean, we studied basic challenge moves and combat as pups, but then we heard about everything Maddie went through, and Lily was kidnapped. Lily! She's always seemed so much tougher than me and that just got me thinking. Then there was the Larkens' attack against Lizzy and multiple attacks against Thomas. I just want to know I can handle myself if something like that happens to me."

I could see this was something that had been weighing heavily on the girl. These were more words than I heard her say the entire night combined.

"You're welcome to join us anytime," I told her. "It will be good for Ruby to have you to spar with." I meant that, too. I had to hold back when we fought, and the enemy would not. Peyton would be a closer match to her skill level and if it brought peace to her sister's mind, then it was a win all around.

"How long were you watching? I can walk you through the steps," Ruby offered.

"If you go slow, I think I have them memorized," she surprised me by saying.

I stood back and let Ruby do the teaching. Peyton was a quick study and by their second round she had the motions down flawlessly.

"Why are we doing these?" Peyton asked. "I mean, I get they are blocking and tackle moves, but why aren't we doing them against each other?"

"Muscle memory," Ruby said. "And boy will your muscles remind you in the days to come."

I laughed aloud as they worked through another set. It drew the attention of a few of the others, and Cole and Elizabeth soon joined me on the sidelines.

"What's going on?" Elizabeth asked.

"I'm teaching Ruby to defend herself," I explained. "And apparently Peyton, too."

Cole chuckled. "So you are feeling rather possessive with a strong need to protect your mate."

I shrugged, unable to deny his accusations and not willing to explain my reasonings. He could think what he wanted.

"How does walking through the motions help prepare them for anything?" Lizzy asked.

"It's a classic battle concept. He's basically training their muscles in the necessary motions, so when the time comes and they need to make that block or attack, their brains know exactly what to do and how to respond," Cole told her. "It's a solid theory. Patrick trains all our Pack in a similar way. After the Bulgarian attack he's made sure every wolf in Westin Pack knows how to fight and defend our territory."

It did not go unnoticed how he interjected himself as Westin Pack. I thought he had aligned with Collier and was transitioning over, but it did not sound that way now. If Cole was still that connected with the Westins, then I needed to be getting on his good side quickly. Maybe he was the connection I needed to get to Kelsey, and not Thomas.

Ruby

Chapter 12

"Bran, what's next?" I hollered over to him.

He had a strange look on his face as he spoke with Cole, and seemed to have tuned out everything else around him.

"Huh?" I heard him say before turning to watch us.

I raised my arms out to my sides in an exaggerated shrug.

"Sorry. One more time through and then I'll have you square off against each other. Slowly," he added.

I rolled my eyes as Pey and I walked through the kata one last time. My muscles were warmed up now and no longer rebelling against each motion.

Our audience continued to grow, and Lily walked in to join Lizzy and Cole. Bran gave his instructions clearly. Truth was, he was an excellent instructor, and I didn't want to ask how he knew some of the things he was teaching me. Something told me the answers would terrify me.

While my mate was loving and caring, there was also an edge to him, a darkness. Sometimes he looked sad, like the weight of the world rested on his shoulders. I really could not care less about whether I learned to fight. There were people in our Pack already assigned to such duties, and I didn't live in fear over the things that had happened to my sisters the way that Peyton apparently did.

I had always taken pride in being able to fend for myself and stand up for myself, but truth was, no one had ever pushed me to the point of actually fighting. My quick wit and sharp tongue were enough to put anyone in their place, and I had learned that lesson at a young age and always used it for my personal benefit.

Bran had Peyton and me square off with each other. He had me start the kata at the midway point and Peyton from the beginning as we faced one another. I laughed at first, thinking it would be sheer chaos and we'd just run into each other. Instead, it was a perfect orchestration. Her advances met my blocks in a synchronized pattern that astonished me.

When I reached the end, he told me to keep going for another round, and my moves flawlessly met Peyton's movements as we switched to her blocking and me attacking.

"That was so cool," Pey squealed when we had completed two full passes. "How did you do that?"

My wolf awoke on edge. My sister was gushing over my mate, and even though I knew it was only in her excitement over the drill, I didn't seem to be able to convince my wolf of that.

Lizzy stepped forward and wrapped a protective arm around my shoulders. "Deep breaths. You got this. Just keep your cool and remember, you're in charge, Ruby. Breathe in, breathe out. Unfortunately, I know that look all too well," she said.

"What look?" I demanded, still feeling far too aggressive.

She smiled knowingly with a patience that I wanted to knock off of her smug face.

"The look of someone about to lose their shit for no reason. You know Peyton isn't even flirting with Bran, Ruby. You know this, but that look says you're about to attack her and for real this time."

I shook my head, trying to deny it, but blood was coursing through my veins and my vision was clouding as my wolf surged to gain control.

Bran saw what was happening and joined us. "I got you," he said confidently, wrapping his arms around my waist.

I turned and buried my face in his chest, breathing in his scent. That smell combined with his touch instantly soothed my wolf.

"Are you okay?" Peyton asked.

I turned my head, a little embarrassed, and smiled. "I'm fine."

As soon as Bran loosened his hold on me, Lily grabbed me and pulled me into a hug. "It sucks sometimes, right?"

We both laughed. I equally hated and loved that my mated sisters understood what I was going through. I knew now that I definitely didn't get it when I jumped in and tried to give advice and tell them they were crazy for mating so quickly. Karma could be a bitch and I was just grateful my sisters were more gracious than I had ever been.

Gage poked his head into the room. "Ruby, everyone, Clara just called Doc back, Mellie's progressing."

There was a celebratory feeling in the room as we headed back into the stables and watched and waited. Mellie wasn't just restless now; a yellowish-colored sac was bulging from her, a clear sign she was close to delivery. Doc and Clara had asked that we keep to the blanketed areas and not approach the mother cow. I wanted to be there with her, but even more than that I wanted what was best for Mellie.

Davidson, our usual veterinarian, arrived with a small team of staff that would tend to the young calves immediately following birth. Davidson, Doc, and Clara patiently waited, assisting when needed until we saw two feet protruding. Soon a little nose poked out.

The miracle of a new birth never ceased to amaze me, and I didn't even try to hold back the tears that flowed as a new life entered the world. Bran held me close, in awe of what he was witnessing for the first time. No one said a word as we all watched in wonder.

I wanted to cheer when the little one dropped, hitting the ground and collapsing. Normally we would leave the babe there to stumble around until it could stand on its own, but since a second was on the way, the vet team swooped in and pulled it away, but still in sight of Mellie so not to stress her any more than necessary.

"It's a boy!" someone announced, and we quietly cheered. I was hoping for two new heifers, but as long as they were both healthy, I didn't really care.

Clara shushed us all as the second baby started to make an appearance. I noticed immediately that its feet were pointed in the wrong direction. I gasped and gripped Bran's hand.

"We have a breach," Clara confirmed seconds later.

"That's what I was afraid of," Davidson calmly said. "Don't worry, Ruby girl, we'll have another healthy baby for you to dote over soon. This isn't our first breach."

I knew he was trying to reassure me, because the last breach birth we had ended badly and I had been devastated. It was pretty common knowledge that I adored the animals and would do anything for them. Bran already knew that, and if he'd had any doubts, they had already been put to rest throughout the night. I loved the fact that he hadn't once complained or questioned my decision to stay the night to be there for Mellie.

I watched with bated breath as Clara, Doc, and Davidson worked to free the second calf. They had to wait until the head started to peek before they could assist with the delivery. The second that happened though, they sprang into action.

"Ruby, Bran, come on over here and give us a hand," Clara called.

I didn't hesitate as I jumped up and walked towards them, Bran close on my heels.

"What can we do?" he asked when I was unable to speak, still worried about the calf.

"I need you each on one side and as we pull, you're going to watch the head and help gently lower the baby to the ground. What we don't want to happen is have the calf drop head first," Clara explained.

I had helped deliver all sorts of animals before, but the excitement and nerves never ceased. I knew all the things that could go wrong in the next few minutes. Fortunately, that wasn't the case this time. Doc issued orders and Clara and Davidson literally pulled the calf from Mellie while Bran and I supported its head and guided it safely to the ground.

The calf immediately made cute little noises and squirmed around, trying to get off its back.

The vet team swarmed in, reuniting the firstborn who was already standing on wobbly legs and ready to try to suckle from Mellie.

"It's a girl!" someone shouted and this time there was no reserve in celebration as everyone cheered and I cried like a freaking baby.

Bran hugged me close. "That was amazing. I'm so proud of you."

I beamed back up at him.

"Thank you for letting me be a part of this. I've never experienced anything like it."

Both calves appeared healthy with good weights. Nearly all my siblings surrounded us, supporting something that was important to me. That made the night pretty close to perfection in my book.

After another hour of monitoring the newborn calves and watching them successfully nurse, people started showing signs of exhaustion. Lily and Thomas apologized and said goodnight, with Shelby and Peyton right behind them.

"If you don't mind me working with you, I'd love to come over on my nights off and work on fighting skills some more," Peyton said hopefully.

I wondered if she was still worried about my outburst of jealousy.

"I'd really like that," I told her honestly.

Lizzy and Cole headed back to Clara's, but Clara and Gage hung around a little longer, even after Doc, Davidson, and the team of vets called it a night. I knew that meant there was no foreseeable threat and the babies had been given an all-clear, but they were so tiny, and I wasn't ready to just let them be.

It was four in the morning when Clara finally declared them perfect and apologized. She was exhausted and couldn't keep her eyes open any longer. I offered her my apartment to sleep a few hours before trying to drive home, but Gage had been sleeping on a bale of hay for a while and was rested enough to get them back home safely. I hugged them both and thanked Clara a thousand times.

Bran hadn't once dozed off, though I could see how tired he was. He just smiled and pushed on right by my side. My heart swelled with love. *Love?* Just love. It happened quickly, but somewhere amidst the madness of the night I had let go of any barriers between us and I was falling helplessly in love with my mate.

I sat down on one of the blankets and he joined me. Mellie and the babies were on the other side of the room as they happily nursed and gained confidence on their legs. Bran took a seat beside me and I rested my head on his shoulder as his arm wrapped around me. He turned and kissed the top of my head as I sighed.

"That was freaking amazing. You were incredible," he said.

I beamed with pride but tried to shove off his compliment. "I bawled like a baby. I rarely ever cry, except where these guys are concerned."

"You truly love the animals," he said.

I wasn't one to hold back my thoughts or my feelings. I turned to look at him and smiled. "I do. I love you, too," I said, before closing the gap between us to seal my words with a kiss.

Bran

Chapter 13

I froze. This wasn't supposed to be happening. The toothpaste, the clothes. I'd even left the toilet seat up knowing how much it would upset her, yet here she was confessing her love for me? My heart soared in happiness, but gloom filled me as I understood the impact of what I'd done. Hearing her say the words aloud made everything so much worse.

Still, when her lips touched mine, nothing else in the entire world mattered but my mate. I pulled her onto my lap and let her straddle me as she deepened the kiss. I pulled back and dared to look around.

"Are there any cameras in here?" I asked her.

"No, none," she said with a devilish grin.

"Good," I said with a growl as I tore her clothes from her body. I needed to see her, touch her, and feel the love she freely offered me. "So beautiful," I told her as I caressed her exposed, soft skin.

I leaned back against the hay. Her steady hands slowly unbuttoned my shirt and pushed it aside to explore my torso muscles. She leaned down and licked and nibbled little paths of pleasure that lighted my body on fire.

"*Po dyavolite*," I swore in Bulgarian.

She grinned as she fumbled with the zipper of my jeans while continuing to torment me. Then she stood up. I hated the cold brushing across my skin at her loss, but I smiled up at her and moved to dispose of my pants.

"Be right back," she said, and disappeared into the next room.

I was confused, but my jaw dropped open when she returned with a cowgirl hat. She quickly got rid of the last of her tattered clothes and then gave me a wink as she secured the hat on top of her head.

She stood between my legs wearing nothing but that hat. I suddenly felt like I was starring in my best wet dream ever as her fingers skimmed along my stomach, letting her nails scrape just enough to cause my skin to prick all over. Then she leaned forward and straddled me.

I moaned in excitement and pulled her closer for a kiss. My hands rubbed up and down her legs as my heart started beating faster. She positioned herself just right and slid slowly onto my length until our bodies were joined as one.

She pulled back with a seductive smirk and rode me like a cowgirl. I had never experienced anything so erotic and in my excitement, I couldn't hold out long. I played with her nipples, and rubbed her to help spur her on, but soon every muscle in my body was tightening and I exploded harder than I'd ever come before. It triggered Ruby's orgasm as she shattered in my arms.

She collapsed against my heaving chest. My heart was beating fast and a sheen of sweat covered my body. I held her tightly as the adrenaline began to wane. My limbs suddenly felt heavy as the weight of the night sunk in.

"What time is it?" she asked, unable to lift her head.

I looked at my watch. "Five-twenty," I confirmed.

"Shit!" she said, jumping up.

I immediately missed the warmth of her body pressed against me. She started gathering up our clothes and offered me her hand to hoist me up. I groaned, not wanting to go anywhere.

Ruby giggled. "We have to get out of here. People will be showing up any second."

My wolf growled as I looked around. I moved quickly, not wanting anyone to see my mate in the state of ecstasy I'd just had her in. I gathered up the last of our things and we ran into the barn and up the stairs to the apartment just as the first truck pulled up. I could hear voices below as I shut the door.

We stood there breathing hard until Ruby began to laugh. I pulled her into my arms as I leaned against the door and laughed with her.

"That was a close one," she said.

"That was worth it," I told her, enjoying the blush that crept across her skin.

"Don't you start that again," she warned. "I need to take a shower and get to work."

I scowled at her. "No. You've been up all night. Take a shower if you need, but you're going to crawl your sexy ass into bed and get some sleep."

"Bran, I can't. I have work to do."

"Clay can handle it," I insisted. I had caught up on the "who's who" list around the ranch and knew Clay was the right man for the job. "Hit the shower and I'll go make sure everything's in order."

"It's my job. I have to work," she stubbornly insisted.

"No, you don't. There's an entire town running this place, Ruby. It doesn't have to all fall onto your shoulders."

"But the dairy—"

I cut her off. "The dairy has an entire team at your disposal. It's well known that you work more hours and harder than anyone here. Let them do their jobs and pitch in."

She pushed away from me, still grumbling under her breath as she headed for the bathroom and slammed the door closed behind her.

I shook my head and couldn't help but grin at my tenacious mate.

I took a moment to throw on some clothes and then headed back downstairs. Clay was already there talking to the team and handing out assignments. He nodded my way when he saw me standing there. As soon as he was done, he walked over.

"Hey," I said.

"Hey. Heard you guys had a long night but the new calves arrived safe and sound. I'm sure Ruby is over the moon about that."

I smiled. "She is. And she hasn't been to sleep yet, but she's taking a shower and determined to be down to work in a few minutes."

He shook his head. "I'm not surprised. She has this thing where no one can do her job for her or as good as her. Mostly she just has this need to prove she's the best and doesn't seem to realize no one questions that point. We all know how good she is and how much she loves the animals, but it doesn't matter who or how many people tell her that. It's never enough."

I frowned. "Yeah, I believe that. Be honest with me, do you need her this morning?"

"No. She'll fuss, but I've already given out the assignments and everyone was in early, excited about the birth of the babies anyway. I can do her walk through and run through her checklist. It's not a problem if you think you can actually get her to stay away." He laughed, knowing that was going to be the hardest part.

I grinned. "We'll see."

"Good luck," Clay said as I headed off to find Wyatt.

"Look what the cat dragged in. You look like shit. Heard you pulled an all-nighter with Ruby last night. Didn't expect to see your face around here today," Wyatt teased.

"Good. That's what I was hoping you'd say. I could probably handle the day but getting Ruby to actually sleep will be difficult and if I leave, she will, too. She's still got a little adrenaline from the night, but I can tell she's on the verge of crashing and I really don't want her to push too hard when it's not necessary."

"Amen to that," Thomas said from behind me. I turned to look at him, knowing I must be tired to have not even heard him approach. "My sister is going to fight you tooth and nail over this, you know."

"I know, but at least you went home for a few hours. She just went upstairs long enough to shower and change. I'm trying to make sure everything's in order before she gets out. I can see how exhausted she is, but I know she'll push on anyway."

Truth was, I was worried about her and highly impressed and proud of her. I'd met few people in my life with the commitment and work ethic my mate held herself to.

"Tell her I'm officially giving you both the day off," Thomas said. "You okay with that, Wyatt? I can ride with you if you need an extra hand."

"Not necessary, it's been quiet out there, boss. And I hear y'all had quite the late night party. You should probably take it easy today, too."

"You're probably right, but at least I got a few hours of sleep. I should be okay," Thomas said before turning back to me. "You think you can manage to keep Ruby home today?"

"I'll do my best," I promised with a grin. I knew ways to ensure she'd stay home, but whether I could get her to actually sleep was the bigger question.

"Something tells me he won't have any problems keeping that girl in bed," Wyatt said with a wink. "Y'all take care. Some of us have to work today."

I said goodbye to Thomas a few minutes later and made my way back up to the apartment. Ruby was in the kitchen making coffee, already dressed and ready for the day.

"Where'd you go?" she asked.

"To check in with everyone for you. Clay has everything under control. Let him do his job. Spoke with Wyatt and Thomas, too. We both have the day off. Boss's orders."

She was already protesting when I reached over and turned off the coffee pot and swooped her up into my arms.

"Bran, I have work to do. Stop it," she squealed.

"Sleep, Ruby. You need sleep more," I insisted as I reached the bedroom and plopped her down on the bed unceremoniously.

"This isn't funny," she huffed.

"It's not meant to be," I said as I stripped out of my clothes and left them in a pile on the floor. I saw her nose flare and eyes widen at the sight. I couldn't help it. I laughed. "I swear I'm putting those back on later. I just put them on, they're still clean."

I could see the redheaded temper flaring. But she didn't pull back when I approached her. I seductively removed her clothes and got no real pushback. Depositing them on the floor next to mine, I pulled the covers back and slid in next to her. She curled into me and sighed.

"I don't appreciate being bullied like this."

I kissed the top of her head. "I know. I'll try not to make a habit of it."

She sighed one last time and within moments she was snoring in my arms.

I grinned down at her sleeping form, thankful she hadn't tried to put up a fight. I closed my eyes and let sleep pull me under.

Ruby

Chapter 14

Bran was right to make me sleep. I wasn't ready to admit that to him, but I would have been worthless throughout the day. He was also right to wake me up after only four hours of sleep, despite my protests.

We visited Mellie and the calves, then went over to Cole and Lizzy's to help with cleanup. I was exhausted by dinner time and barely touched my food. Still, he insisted that I walk through my exercises five times before taking a shower and finally collapsing into bed.

When I awoke the next day, I felt like my normal self; still, I wasn't about to admit he was right.

Bran and I fell into a comfortable routine. Each evening was spent with him helping Cole and Gage while I either spent time with the new babies or hanging out with my sisters. We would meet up for a late dinner, then go through our workouts. Peyton would join in on her evenings off, and we started sparring more. But the best part of every day was making love with my gorgeous mate until we were both fully sated and then drifting off to sleep.

When the weekend rolled around, I knew there was one thing I still had to do—introduce Bran to Mom and Dad. I had been ignoring Mom's calls and delaying this moment. I didn't really know why, though. Bran got along great with all my siblings. He was holding his own around the ranch and everyone seemed to like him. But I had never introduced a guy to my parents. Not once, ever.

"Why are you so nervous about this?" Bran asked as we were finishing getting ready to head over to the Alpha house for dinner.

"I don't know. Honestly, I don't know. I've never brought anyone home to meet the family before," I told him. "And you're like the forever serious thing."

"I already know everyone there but your parents," he reminded me.

"I know, I know. But these are my parents. I want them to like you as much as I do."

"And you don't think they will?"

"How do I know? This is all new territory for me."

Bran laughed. "I think you're stressing out over nothing, sweetheart. Besides, shouldn't I be the one nervous here?"

"Yes, so why aren't you?"

He laughed and kissed me. "You're impossible, and everything is going to be just fine."

"I know I'm being unreasonable and silly here. It just feels like a big moment," I said, trying to explain what I was feeling and butchering it badly.

"Come on. Let's just get this over with then, sooner rather than later. Hopefully when we get there, you'll calm down some."

I shrugged. "I wouldn't count on it, my family always makes me a little psychotic," I muttered under my breath.

We left the apartment and got in the truck to make the short drive into town. It dawned on me that Bran already knew many in our Pack from working at the ranch. I made a mental note to go into town with him soon as we really hadn't done that yet. I didn't want him to feel like I was embarrassed by him or anything. I didn't particularly enjoy the sort of attention a new mate brought. It really had nothing to do with him.

Bran pulled up to the house and I sat there looking at it. It had been a good place to grow up. Collier Pack in general was. It made me stop and think about the children Bran and I would someday have—not too soon of course, but someday.

My door opened and Bran stood there staring at me.

"Penny for your thoughts?"

I blushed. "You don't want to know."

"Come on. You know you can tell me anything."

"No secrets between mates," I said and thought I saw him cringe just a little. He recovered quickly so I assumed I'd just imagined it.

"What's on your mind tonight, Red?"

I smiled and wrapped my arms around his neck. "I was just thinking of this house and growing up here and imagining what our children will be like someday." That time I definitely saw him cringe. "I'm not saying we have to have kids, at least not right away, but someday I'd like to think we will."

Bran stared at me and I immediately regretted saying anything, then he softened and kissed me. "I can't imagine anything greater than a houseful of our children."

"Really?" I asked.

"Really."

"Hey! You guys gonna stand out here making out all night, or are you actually coming in for dinner?" Lily yelled from the front door.

I buried my face in his chest and said a quick prayer that this evening would go by swiftly. Taking his hand, I jumped down and we walked into the house.

"Nice. Real subtle there, Lily," Bran said.

She shrugged happily. "No pretense here, Bran. You'll learn quickly."

Lily led us back to the dining room where dinner was already on the table and everyone was waiting. Mom and Dad rose and met us at the door.

"Um, Mom, Dad, this is my mate, Bran. Bran, these are my parents. Cora and Zach Collier."

Bran shook hands with my father, and Mom had tears in her eyes when she hugged him. The introductions were quick, and my parents didn't make a fuss about it at all. That surprised me a lot. Bran took the seat next to Dad and throughout dinner they talked casually. No one interrogated him or teased me in any way. It was weird and set me on edge.

"What's going on? Why is everyone being so nice and cordial tonight?" I asked Lizzy as we cleared the table to make room for dessert.

She laughed. "You can thank Peyton for that. Oh trust me, most of us were ready for some good payback tonight, but she begged us to back off and be nice. Said you were really nervous about introducing Bran to Mom and Dad. We have plenty of time to razz you both later. Besides, everyone feels like we already know him and so what's the fun in interrogating at this point?"

I hugged her. "Thank you."

"Thank Peyton," she said.

"Oh, I intend to. I was a nervous wreck coming here tonight."

Lizzy smiled. "I get it. It's big, real, or more real somehow officially introducing him to the family. I mean, everyone knew Cole already and had for years, but introducing him as my mate was really tough."

"I'm sorry if I made it harder."

"You did, but I love you anyway," she said.

I started to finally relax after that, and the evening went by smoothly. Dad and Bran seemed to connect well, and Mom pulled me aside before we left to tell me how wonderful he was. I felt like I could finally breathe a little easier and apologized to her for not bringing him by to meet them sooner.

I pulled Peyton aside as everyone was saying goodbyes.

"Thank you. Lizzy told me what you did," I said, giving her a big hug. "I didn't deserve it."

She shrugged. "I know, but this was important, and I knew you were stressing about it. Besides, like I told them, Bran's already part of the family anyway so anything said or done would have just been vengeance towards you, and that wasn't how sisters should be."

"You're the best!" I said as Bran and Cole finished their conversation and we left for home.

"See, I don't know why you were so worried," he said as he helped me into the truck.

I groaned. "You have no idea."

We headed home and the next day kicked off just like any other. I worked; I had lunch with Bran; and then after work, he stopped in long enough to say hi before heading over to Cole and Lizzy's. They had the place dried out and the destroyed flooring pulled up, but the next few days would be spent laying the new floors.

He wasn't gone even an hour when Clara called and told me to get my butt over to her house ASAP.

"I have a surprise for you," she said.

We hung up the phone and I jumped in the truck and drove straight over to Clara's. Before I could even knock on her front door it flew open and I was pulled inside.

"What the hell is going on?" I asked.

"Surprise," Kelsey said as she threw her arms in the air.

"Kelsey? What are you doing here?" I asked, excited to see our friend from Westin Pack.

"Kyle came to help Cole, so I tagged along. Mary's watching the boys, so this is like our first trip away from them since little Jason was born," she said.

I crossed the room and threw my arms around her.

"It's so great to see you!"

Kelsey and I had grown close after Cole and Elizabeth were attacked. Cole had nearly lost his life and suffered severe burns that had them both in the hospital for several months. Being fully bonded, Lizzy had suffered alongside him through it all.

The institution they were taken to was close to Westin Pack so anytime I visited, which was often, I got to spend time with Kelsey and really got to know her. After that she had quickly become an honorary Collier sister. I hadn't seen her in several months and was thrilled with their spontaneous visit.

"I hear you have a handsome new mate," she said.

I grinned, just thinking of Bran. "That I do. I can't wait for you to meet him."

"I can't wait. I'm so happy for you. Clara tells me he's your one true mate."

I sighed. "Yes, he is."

"Aww, you guys, I think Ruby has fallen in love," Lizzy teased.

I gave her a strange look. "What?"

"You do sound like a woman in love," Kelsey said.

"And why shouldn't I be? He's my mate. Of course I love him," I said.

"Wow, she admitted to that quickly," Clara said.

"Just because you mated him doesn't necessarily mean you fall madly in love right away. Does he know?" Lizzy asked.

I laughed. "Of course he knows."

"I mean, have you actually said the words to him?" she clarified, rolling her eyes.

"Yes, of course I have," I said.

"Wow, I'm impressed. Let's face it, you aren't exactly the 'let's sit around and share our feelings' type, Ruby," Lizzy pointed out.

I shrugged. "Honestly, I learned everything not to do when it comes to mating from you three, and Lily. Where is she tonight?"

"Pack Mother obligations. She's going to try to stop by later tonight, but probably won't see her until tomorrow," Kelsey said.

"How long will you be in town?" I asked Kelsey.

"Just through the weekend."

"Still, it's so great to see you."

My sisters and I sat around chatting late into the night. Gage and Cole came home to shower and collapse in bed. They told us Bran was headed home and Kyle had gone back to the Alpha house, so Kelsey and I said goodnight and headed out together.

"Maybe you and Kyle could come over for dinner one night while you're here," I suggested.

"I would love that. Let's plan on it," she said without setting a definitive date or time.

I headed back to the house, excited to tell Bran all about my evening.

Bran

Chapter 15

When I arrived at Cole's, as I had for several days now, I was prepared to work hard laying the new flooring. Not only was I getting in good with Cole and Gage, but the last two nights Thomas had come by to help.

I was quickly becoming one of the guys. They trusted me to do my part and I had given them no reason to doubt I would. My plan was steadfast: continue getting close to Thomas, and now Cole too, in the hopes that one of them would someday lead me to the witch Elena so I could fulfill my mission.

With Ruby's sudden talk of children when we had gone to dinner at her parents, I was in no rush for that "someday" to occur. I wanted as much time with my mate as I could selfishly get, but I knew the blood oath would kick in the moment I was near the witch.

Nothing could have prepared me for that moment to come now.

I received a shock as I walked in to Cole's place only to be greeted by none other than Kyle Westin. He already knew exactly who I was, too.

"Hey, man, you must be Bran. I'm Kyle. I'm just in town to help out for a few days."

I didn't dare ask if his mate was with him. I had no plan of attack prepared. I had assumed if she were to come to Collier that there would be advance notice, but apparently that was not the case.

I kept my head down and listened as the men talked while we worked. I stayed quiet and let them catch up, or at least Cole, Thomas, and Kyle. Turned out Gage had yet to meet the Alpha of Westin before now, either.

With the five of us working, we knocked out more than we had completed in any given night. Kyle did not allow his status to keep him from getting his hands dirty, and by the time we agreed to call it a night, I had already begun to respect him.

If this mission was all I cared about then it was the perfect setup. There was even a chance I could get Kelsey alone, kill her quickly, and no one would ever have to know.

But I would know. That wasn't something I could just keep from my mate. Ruby and I were bonded and if I lived long enough that bond would someday seal. When that happened, she would be privy to all my deepest, darkest secrets. She would know, and she would never forgive me.

That one thought and the pain it caused deep in my chest was the only reason I said goodbye, walked outside, stripped from my clothes, and shifted. Then I fought against the blood oath that burned through my veins and turned away from the direction it was calling me and ran home to my redheaded goddess.

The witch's magic was strong, and it hurt, but not as much as the mere thought of destroying Ruby by my actions. I knew that should I ever come in close contact with Kelsey, things would be all the worse and harder to walk away from, but for now I shifted back, changed into my clothes, and walked into my apartment to hold my mate.

"Hey." She greeted me at the door with a kiss.

I held her tightly, never wanting to let her go.

"You okay?" she asked.

I smiled against her neck where she bore my bond mark. I took a deep breath, inhaling her scent then blowing mine onto her neck, causing her to shiver.

"I am now."

We didn't go through her workout that night. Instead, I carried her straight to bed and made love to her, losing myself in my mate until all the pain had disappeared.

The next morning I awoke with a feeling of dread. Kelsey was somewhere in Collier at that very moment. I didn't know how to avoid her or what would happen if our paths crossed. I was still working with Wyatt and we had two days left out riding the range. I said a prayer that Kelsey did not choose today to go for a horse ride.

When it was time to head back in for lunch, I made up an excuse to Wyatt and stayed out on my own contemplating my options. The oath would only grow stronger and more impatient the closer I got to Kelsey and the longer she stayed in Collier territory.

I stayed out as late as I could on the range, then headed back in with a prayer she wasn't in the area. My prayers were answered. The blood in my veins told me she wasn't nearby, but I could feel my mate's presence. I made a beeline for the apartment, called Cole to apologize for not making it, and surprised Ruby with a night she would not soon forget.

I felt I was on borrowed time now and there were a few fantasies of my own I wanted to fulfill first.

The next morning my muscles ached, but I couldn't wipe the smile from my face, and all I had to do was look at Ruby to cause a blush to spread across her cheeks, down her neck, and over her chest. It was a beautiful sight.

I went to work as usual and again stayed out when Wyatt went in for lunch. I came back a little earlier in the day, though. As I was cooling down my horse, Austin was preparing two horses for riders. My skin grew cold when I heard him mention they were for Kelsey and Kyle.

I had to get out of there, but an opening came when Austin got called away. My blood boiled and I knew I had to act quickly. I looked down, spotting a few burrs on my pants. I removed them and chose the smaller of the horses as my victim. Something told me that would be the one Kelsey rode. I felt nauseous as I loosened the saddle and placed a few of the burrs just on the underside.

I left the scene and headed straight for the apartment. Looking at the time I knew Ruby wouldn't be home for a few more hours. Knowing Kelsey was definitely going to be in the area, I began to freak out a little.

I went to the bathroom and drew a hot bath. Most wolf shifters hated artificial smells, or even just strong scents because of our sensitive noses, but there was this one smelly bath salt that Ruby loved. I dumped a handful into the water, then a second for good measure. I scrunched up my nose at the stench that assailed me as I stripped from my clothes and settled into the water.

Next, I grabbed my cell phone. Seating my earbuds in place, I cranked up some music to play as loudly as I could stand it. My hope was that if I couldn't smell or hear Kelsey nearby, I could fight the urge to track and kill her.

The water was just starting to cool when my eyes shot open as Ruby slid into the tub to hover over me. I pushed up to kiss her. I couldn't hear anything, and my senses were distorted from the overpowering smell of the bath salts, but I could see her, and my hands could feel her as they skimmed over her wet body.

I leaned forward enough to take one of her nipples into my mouth, as I teased it with my teeth and tongue. She wasted no time positioning herself over my stiff shaft and lowering herself onto me. She sat there for a moment as I continued to tease her until neither of us could stand it any longer, then began to move.

One thing I had learned was my sassy beauty liked to be on top, but she liked me to be in charge. My hands rested on her hips as I guided her body, setting the pace of her movements to the beat of the drum pounding through the song playing in my ears. I didn't know a lot of things in life, but I knew exactly how to please my woman. As I felt myself swelling impossibly harder, I toyed with her in just the erotic places she responded to the fastest, and soon she threw her head back and I saw her body shake all over triggering my own orgasm, just as the song ended and a slower one began.

I wasn't sure how long I'd been in the tub, or if it was safe to remove the earbuds, but I loved the sweet little noises of appreciation Ruby made after sex and decided it was worth the risk. Popping them out, I was greeted by the sounds of my very satisfied mate.

"I don't know what brought that on, but I will leave work early every day if this is the reward I get," I said in a husky voice that made her body quake.

"Mmm, I could be okay with that," she finally said. "I'm almost sorry we don't have the whole evening alone like this."

"I could ditch Cole's tonight and we could stay right here," I offered.

"Lizzy stopped by and said to tell you that Cole needed to make another supply run tonight, so you have the night off. I invited

Kelsey and Kyle over for dinner the second I heard. I know you've met Kyle already, and I'm certain you're going to just love Kelsey to death."

I tried to reign in my shock at her eerily appropriate terminology, when her phone rang. She growled in frustration but got out of the tub to retrieve it. I hated to see her leave, but I sure did enjoy the view, even in my state of shock.

"Hey Clara," she said answering the phone. "What? Are you kidding? Is she okay? Okay, yeah, of course. If you guys need anything just let us know. I know she's already in the best of care. Send her my love."

Ruby hung up the phone and looked at it sadly.

"What's wrong?" I asked.

"There was an accident on Kelsey and Kyle's ride. The horse got spooked and threw her. She wasn't prepared for it and broke her leg during the fall. Kyle carried her back to Clara's. She was able to set it, and Kelsey will be fine, but obviously they aren't coming tonight now."

"I'm sorry, sweetheart. I know how much you were looking forward to it."

Relief washed over me. Was it because Kelsey wasn't coming? Or because I had only injured her? I suddenly realized I didn't want to kill the witch. She meant too much to my mate, but it didn't matter, because my Alpha still wanted her dead and I was bound by blood to see that through.

Ruby

Chapter 16

I felt terrible for Kelsey and the next morning I got up and went down to start my day, but instead of issuing orders and diving into work, I asked Clay to take over for me. He had really been stepping up to the plate lately and helping out. Bran was right. I didn't have to do it all. We were a team and I would be a better leader if I started acting like it.

As my guys gathered around for daily assignments, instead of barking orders, I shocked them all.

"Clay," I said.

"Yes, ma'am."

I passed him the clipboard. "Please give out assignments and see that our milk supply runs on time today."

"You sure?" he asked, hesitantly.

I smiled. "I have full confidence in you. I have a few personal things to take care of this morning," I said. I think that surprised them even more. I never took personal time off, except for the days after Bran came into my life.

"But, Ruby, Bran already headed out for the day. I spoke to him a few minutes ago," Austin said.

"Austin," Clay said in a threatening tone that meant "Shut the hell up."

I laughed. "I didn't mean that kind of personal stuff. Kelsey and Kyle are visiting, and she was thrown from one of our horses last night, broke her leg. I'd like to go and check on my friend and I am confident in Clay's leadership skills to hold down the fort here for a few hours."

Austin grinned. "About damn time. That boy's been working his ass off for a promotion."

I groaned. "I didn't say promotion . . . yet." I turned to Clay and gave him an encouraging smile. "We'll talk soon, though."

With that, I turned to leave. There was excitement as the guys congratulated Clay. He'd practically been doing more of my job than I had for the last few weeks, but I could see how my public praise of him would mean more than I expected for all of them.

By the time I drove over to Clara's I actually felt relaxed. I'd been thinking a lot about the future. Ever since I'd mentioned someday wanting kids, it had opened my heart to something I had never known I wanted.

I'd worked hard my entire life to fit in with the boys and hold my own. I always had something to prove to myself and to them, or that's what it had felt like. I had made it clear I wasn't one of the boys, only that I was just as good as them.

Now with Bran in my life, I suddenly didn't feel like I had anything more to prove. My goals were changing directions. I was the last of my sisters anyone would suspect to want the big crazy family, but the more I thought of it, the more I knew that was exactly what I wanted.

And I knew I would give up working eventually to have that. Me, a stay-at-home mom. I laughed out loud at the thought. No one would ever believe it. Relinquishing some of my duties to Clay felt like a first step in that direction, though, and I felt good about it.

I parked in front of Clara's and practically bounced to the front door. I knocked but didn't wait for her to answer before walking in.

"Clara?" I hollered.

"Kitchen," she yelled back.

I walked in and found Kelsey sitting at the kitchen table with her leg casted and propped up on the chair across from her.

"Hey, Kels. Wanted to come by and check on you," I said. I leaned down and gave her a hug and took the empty chair next to her. "How's the leg?"

111

"Fine. I just feel like an idiot that it happened at all. You'd think I'd never ridden a horse before or something."

"Had you?"

"No, but that's not the point," she said with a laugh.

"You'll have to excuse her. She was in a lot of pain still this morning, so Kyle asked if I'd give her some painkillers, and let's just say that Kelsey is the equivalent of a lightweight drunk," Clara explained.

"I bet she's been a lot of fun this morning," I said.

Clara laughed. "Yeah, she has. Lizzy should be back soon. I think she's picking Lily up on her way back. I didn't think to call you because I thought you'd be working. Why aren't you working?"

I shrugged. "I passed it off to Clay for today and wanted to come check on Kelsey. I'm thinking of giving him a promotion and lessening my load some."

I tried to play it off as no big deal, but it was a very big deal and the surprised look on Clara's face told me she thought so, too.

"Um, wow, that's great. Any particular reason for this change?" she prodded.

"No," I insisted.

"Are you pregnant?" Kelsey blurted out. "I mean, you're much more of a workaholic than I ever was, but when we started talking about having a family, I started pulling back from my duties at work."

"So, are you pregnant?" Clara asked.

"Wait, who's pregnant?" Lily demanded as she and Lizzy walked in.

"No one's pregnant," I said. "This has nothing to do with babies or a family," I insisted.

"Then what are we talking about?" Lily asked as she stood in the doorway with one hand on her hip.

"Touchy subject," Kelsey warned. "Lily and Thomas have been trying for a few months now."

"What?" I asked. "Why didn't you say anything?"

"Because we aren't trying. We're just talking about maybe trying sometime in the future."

"Lily wants a baby so bad she can't stand it, but Thomas isn't ready yet, too stressed and still adjusting to his new Alpha roles."

"Would you shut up already?" Lily scolded Kelsey. "I told you that in confidence. What is wrong with you?"

Clara giggled. "Sorry. It's the painkillers. I'm sure she doesn't mean it. It's been a lot like having you around all morning, Lil—no filter!"

I laughed because it was true. Lily never sugarcoated anything. She was as transparent as a person could possibly be.

"Well, you guys are welcome to all the babies. I will gladly spoil rotten any and all nieces and nephews, but I am definitely not ready for kids," Lizzy said. "Maybe it's selfish of me, but I don't really care. I waited a long time for my happily ever after and I just want to enjoy my mate for now. Sure, I've had fleeting thoughts of kids, but after the misery we suffered all those years, Cole and I still have a lot of making up to do."

Clara rolled her eyes. "And they do, several times a night."

Lizzy actually blushed as we all laughed.

"How about you, Clara?" I asked.

She shrugged. "Eventually. Gage and I are still adjusting and trying to figure out what our life looks like now. I think we're both getting a little stir-crazy around here and anxious for a new assignment. Honestly, as bad as it sounds, I'm glad your house flooded, Lizzy. Gives Gage something to do while we're home."

It was Lizzy's turn to roll her eyes. "I'm glad my misfortune could help you."

The morning passed quickly as we talked about anything and everything. It was rare that my sisters and I opened up in this way, though it was becoming more common.

As noon approached Clara asked me to run over to the diner and pick up lunch for us all. Peyton was working and had it ready. Of course I said yes. When I arrived, I was surprised to find Bran there having lunch with Wyatt.

"Hey, what are you doing here?" he asked, rising to give me a kiss when he saw me.

"I took the day off, or at least part of it. The girls are over at Clara's entertaining Kelsey, or I suppose she's entertaining us as Clara has her high on painkillers."

Wyatt chuckled. "We don't even want to know."

"Yeah, probably best. I'm just picking up lunch for everyone."

Kate, Wyatt's mate and owner of Kate's Diner, came out to see him. They were too cute together. Bran and Wyatt had seemed to hit it off well and I made a mental note to invite them to dinner sometime soon.

"Peyton's in the back working on a cake. Asked if you mind hanging out for about an hour." Kate said.

I sighed. I had thought I was just swinging by to pick up our food.

"How long do you have left for lunch?" I asked Bran.

"I'm meeting up with Mr. Draper at two, so I have a few hours to blow," he said.

I beamed. "Then I guess it's my lucky day." I took his hand and pulled him up. "We're going to go check in with Peyton and give you two a few minutes alone." I looked around the diner, noting there wasn't an empty seat to be found. "Well, sort of."

Bran and I headed back into the kitchen but didn't see Peyton amongst the hustle of lunch hour.

"Looking for Peyton? She's in the back kitchen," one of the chefs informed me.

"Thanks," I said as Bran and I danced our way through the madness, trying to stay out of everyone's way.

The back kitchen was a small room with a stove and oven set up, a prep table, and a table that generally sat two, but could expand to accommodate up to eight people. It could be booked for special occasions with a chef assigned to prepare food right there as a unique dining experience. Collier didn't exactly have many special date night sort of places, so Wyatt had built that on to the back of the diner to offer something extra to the place. It was booked nearly every night of the week, and months in advance for holidays. Peyton was most often the featured chef and jokingly claimed the kitchen for herself.

"Hey P, Clara said lunch was ready, but Kate said you'd be another hour or so?"

"I'm so sorry. I was trying to get everything in order, but we've been slammed since breakfast. I just wanted to bake a cake for Kelsey."

"That's so sweet. Is lunch ready? I could always come back and pick up the cake in an hour," I offered. "Otherwise I'll be forced to hang out with this guy and ignore our poor sisters."

Bran scowled. "I thought that was already the plan."

"Yeah, but I was going to drop their lunch off first," I said.

"Okay, give me just a minute," Peyton said. We watched as she tossed the wet ingredients into the mixer with the dry ones and turned it on. As soon as it was done, she pulled the beaters up and checked the consistency. Satisfied, she abandoned the cake and I followed her out into the main kitchen to retrieve the subs, cold salads, and chips that Clara had ordered.

I turned to pass some of it off to Bran, but he wasn't there.

"Bran?" I hollered.

He came out of the back kitchen and smiled. "Sorry. Did you need me?"

"Yeah. Can you carry these out to my truck?"

"Sure thing, sweetheart."

He took the trays Peyton handed off to him and walked out. She assured me the cake would be ready in one hour, so I told her I'd see her then, set a timer on my phone so I wouldn't forget and followed Bran out.

Bran

Chapter 17

My heart was racing. That had been close. Seeing that cake batter sitting there and knowing it was for Kelsey, I had to act. My Alpha had given me several vials of poison. It was specially formulated, all natural, no detectable smell or taste. The vials were small and hidden inside my boot for travel—and for moments just like that.

The second Peyton and Ruby left the room, I pulled them out and dumped three into the batter, stirring quickly so it wouldn't be evident. They were designed to put in a teacup; one drink and it would be lights out for good. I didn't know how many vials it would take in a cake or how baking it would affect the composition of the poison, but I had to try.

The fire in my blood had temporarily subsided because of my actions and I felt good again, right up to the moment Ruby called for me, then reality came crashing back.

I walked into the kitchen and took the trays Ruby handed me out to her truck. My body felt heavy with the burden of guilt that set in. I had spent enough time around Kyle Westin to understand why my brother, Nicholai, had not only made a temporary alliance with the man, but also how it had changed his opinions on seeking revenge for our parents' deaths.

Kyle wasn't a bad guy. He had only reacted to protect his mate when my father had attacked his territory and threatened the one person who meant everything to him. I had thought Lily was Thomas's weakness, but hearing the stories he shared with Cole and

Kyle while we'd worked on the floors, I was beginning to understand that while yes, in some ways, a mate was the ultimate vulnerability, she was also a man's biggest strength.

I already knew I would do anything in my power to keep Ruby safe and if someone came into our home, my territory, and threatened my woman, death would be a welcome end for that person. He'd even be begging for it.

My father had to have known that. Perhaps he was too arrogant and believed Kyle too young and untrained to take him. I would never understand for certain, but I couldn't find it in myself to hold a grudge against Kyle for protecting his mate.

The hatred that I had carried for the last few years towards the Westin family had diminished. Nicholai had tried to explain as much to me on his return from Westin Pack after the temporary alliance to fight against the big cats. Many had argued against him going in the first place, but he had assured everyone that it would change nothing, only a temporary peace for the betterment of all wolf shifters as they battled an even bigger enemy.

But he had returned changed. He confided in me that he could no longer in good conscience seek the revenge for our father that everyone wanted. He had tried to explain it to me at the time, and I didn't get it, until now.

There had been a lot of pushback from the Pack and it had opened up an opportunity for my Alpha to step in and divide us. I knew now I had been wrong to follow him. I didn't want to believe it, but Nicholai had been right. If I ever got the chance to tell him that and apologize, I would.

I only had myself to blame for the position I was in, but the longer I managed to keep Kelsey alive, the more time I had with Ruby, and selfishly that was what I wanted. I needed to go back into that kitchen and destroy the cake I'd contaminated.

Just thinking about that caused a sharp pain to slice through my hand where I'd cut myself for the blood oath. I nearly dropped the platters I was carrying and fought not to buckle at my knees. Ruby ran over and opened the door to the truck, and I set them on the front seat.

"Are you okay?" she asked.

My heart was still beating fast. "Fine," I lied. "Just twisted my ankle on the gravel. It's nothing."

I wasn't sure what hurt me more: lying to Ruby or the scorching pain of the oath.

I made up an excuse not to go back to Clara's with her, kissed her goodbye and headed back into the diner with Wyatt.

"You could have ditched me," he joked.

"I know, but that's a lot of estrogen over at that house."

He laughed and nodded in understanding. I knew it would cause too much pain to try and fix the wrong I'd made, so I headed back to the ranch with Wyatt and tried to deny to myself what I'd done.

Mr. Draper stopped me and asked if we could reschedule for the next day, and that meant I was free of work. I needed something to do, so I helped Wyatt and Conlin as they shoveled hay to distribute to the animals. The physical exertion was just what I needed. By mid-afternoon, my aching muscles felt good and I was proud of at least something I'd done that day.

Austin ran into the barn where we were working. He stopped short and looked at me with little color left in his face. It had happened, Kelsey was dead. I knew those would be the next words from his mouth, but I was wrong.

"Bran, come quick. Ruby's awfully sick. Doc says it's food poisoning. Clara, Lizzy, Lily, and Kelsey all have it, too."

I wanted to throw up. The cake was for Kelsey. I had never stopped to consider the others would eat it too. *Ruby!* My heart stopped in my chest.

"Is she okay? Austin, is Ruby okay?"

"I don't know. They can't seem to stop throwing up. Ruby's the worst though. She's in and out of consciousness. It's not good, Bran."

"Where is she? Where is my mate?" I demanded.

"They moved her to your apartment to make her as comfortable as possible."

I took off across the farm at a full run, taking the steps two at a time as I burst into the home we shared. This was all my fault. Ruby wasn't supposed to eat the cake.

My wolf surged and all I could see was red, but the only person I could blame was myself.

Thomas, Lily, and Doc were all inside. Lily looked pale but was standing steadily and didn't look too affected by the poison. I could hear Ruby vomiting in the bathroom. I started to go to her, but Thomas held me back.

"Bran, I need you to calm down before you go in there," he said sternly.

I started to push him out of my way, but I could feel him using his Alpha powers to subdue me.

"I have to go to her, Thomas. I have to see she's okay."

"She's not okay. She's very sick at the moment. Doc thinks it will pass, but she's got to get it out of her system. There's nothing you can do for her."

I ran my fingers through my hair. *Po dyavolite! What had I done?*

I was barely keeping it together as I started to pace.

"You just need to calm down before you see her, is all," Lily said.

I turned to look at her. "Austin said you and the other girls were sick too, but you look fine."

"Clara, Lizzy, Kelsey, and I threw up the worst of it, then shifted to allow our wolves to heal us. I feel a little weak, but I'm fine and haven't thrown up again since I shifted back."

"So why is Ruby still so sick? What happened?"

"I dunno, Bran," Lily said, trying to comfort me the best she could.

Doc came out of the bathroom where he was checking on my mate. I could still hear her violently throwing up.

"Well, I'm afraid it's going to be a long night, son, but Ruby should be fine in a few days," the old man announced.

"A few days? Lily's already healed. What's happening?"

I knew what was happening. Karma was a bitch and she was after me. Ruby was sick because of what I'd done. If I lost her, I didn't know if I was strong enough to go on living and I suddenly felt envious of Cole and Kyle for their sealed bonds, knowing they would never have to face a world without their mates.

Doc smiled at me. "The other girls were able to throw up, shift, and recover. I'm certain it was just a bit of food poisoning, nothing to get too worked up about."

Ruby retched again. "That doesn't sound like nothing, Doc," I insisted, cursing myself for not bringing along an antidote.

"I really don't know how to tell you this, Bran, but Ruby couldn't shift. She's got to just wait it out, so she's going to be sicker a little longer than the others."

My blood went cold. "What? Why couldn't she shift, Doc? I mean, if she's that sick, her wolf should take over and protect her."

"It can't," Doc said.

I started pacing the room again. I was wracking my brain to remember everything I knew about the poison I'd used. I couldn't remember ever hearing of this as a side effect. It made me sick to my stomach and I wanted to throw up, too.

"Promise me she's going to be okay. I've never heard of a sickness that wouldn't allow a person to shift. Her wolf should be protecting her from this," I repeated.

"You're not listening. It can't," Doc said again.

Thomas put his hand on my shoulder, and I jerked away, but he only put it back and squeezed hard enough to get my attention. "You might want to sit down for this."

Sit down? I didn't want to sit down. I had to do something, but there was nothing I could do. I had never in my life felt so helpless. With Thomas guiding me to sit, I obeyed. My shoulders slumped over in defeat and an unimaginable pain set into my chest. I'd failed my mate.

Lily kneeled before me. "Bran, listen to me. What Doc is saying is that when we shifted, Ruby tried to, and she couldn't. She could not call her wolf forward. Now it's still early, but there's only one reason any of us knows of that would cause this."

I looked up into her eyes as tears flooded mine. I shook my head. It wasn't possible.

Thomas squatted next to his mate and smiled. "We believe Ruby's pregnant. Looks like you're gonna be a dad, buddy!"

I sunk back against the couch in complete shock. Pregnant? Ruby was carrying my child? How was that even possible? It had only been a few weeks since we'd met.

"Bran, you okay?" Lily asked, but it sounded like she was off in a great distance. "Doc?"

"Give the boy some time, he's just in a bit of shock."

In the next room Ruby vomited again. I stood and walked towards the noise. I felt like I was having an out-of-body experience, watching myself move, but not feeling a part of it. No one moved to stop me this time.

The bathroom carried a terrible odor, but I didn't care. I fell to my knees by her side and pulled her hair back out of the way as another wave of nausea hit her. When she was through, she took some toilet paper and wiped her mouth before turning to look at me.

A tear ran down my cheek. She was so pale and fragile looking. My eyes shot down to her flat stomach and I watched as my hand reached out to reverently touch it.

"I'm so sorry," I said.

She smiled and shrugged. "I guess they told you both the bad and good news," she said in a hoarse voice, no doubt strained from throwing up so much.

"This is all my fault. I didn't think," I started to ramble, but she quieted me with a radiant smile.

Her hand covered mine where it still rested on her stomach. "It's worth it," she insisted.

I stayed with her through it all, holding back her hair, washing her face, and putting cool rags on the back of her neck to soothe her. Doc left with instructions to call if anything changed or worsened, but Lily and Thomas stayed. They didn't get in the way or hover over Ruby, but they were there, just in the next room through it all.

I tried to tell them it wasn't necessary, but when I went to kick them out they both stubbornly insisted they would do the same for any member of the Pack. While I tended to my mate's needs, they tended to mine. Lily mothered me like no one ever had before, insisting I eat, and drink regularly, reminding me that I wouldn't be able to help Ruby if I let myself get too weak.

For thirty-six hours, my mate continued to vomit until she was only throwing up bile and blood. Doc came back several times to check on her but assured us there was nothing more that could be done. It just had to run its course.

Thomas traded off watching Ruby for me whenever Lily insisted I had to rest. I didn't sleep well, the nightmares and guilt plagued me, but I tried because I knew Lily was right and my body needed the rest. I had to stay strong for Ruby and the baby.

A baby? I was going to be a father. This changed everything, but it also changed nothing. I had never felt so helpless in all my life.

Finally the vomiting ceased and Ruby crumbled to the floor like a wet noodle. I shooed Lily out of the room, ran a hot bath, and carefully lowered her into the water. Bathing and caring for my mate brought me a little peace. She stubbornly insisted she could do it herself, but she had little resistance left in her. Her body was so weak and vulnerable that it had my wolf on full alert.

I lifted her from the water, dried her with a towel, and took one of my shirts to cover her. Once I had her dressed and tucked her into bed, Lily came in. She fussed over her and helped feed her some chicken broth and dry toast she had ready and waiting. Ruby only got a little in her before exhaustion set in and she curled into my side and slept.

"Should we wake her and get a little more food in her system?" Lily asked, clearly as worried as I was.

"No, just put it in the fridge and I'll make sure she eats when she wakes."

"How are you holding up?" Thomas surprised me by asking.

I shrugged. "I'll tell you when I figure that out myself."

He laughed and nodded. "She's stronger than she looks, Bran."

"I know. I just pray the baby survived this. She'd never forgive herself if we lost it."

Lily leaned down and hugged me as she smoothed down Ruby's wet hair. "They're both going to be just fine. I know it."

"I hope you're right," I said honestly. I knew I wouldn't be around much longer for her, but I was happier than I expected to know she wouldn't be alone for the rest of her life. She'd have a piece of me to care for and love. It wasn't the same. It wasn't enough, but it was more than I ever expected I could offer her.

"Call us if you need anything at all," Thomas said. "I'm going to drag Lil out of here and force her to get some sleep now, too."

"I'm not ready to leave her," Lily insisted.

"Come on, slugger. They're just going to be sleeping. You can come back and check on them later."

Reluctantly she said goodbye and let Thomas take her home.

Ruby
Chapter 18

I felt like death. I'm pretty sure there were moments when I had prayed for God to just take me home. I had never been so sick or felt so miserable in my entire life. Kelsey and my sisters had shifted and seemed fine afterwards, but my wolf wouldn't let me shift and I hadn't understood why until they explained it.

Pregnant! I was pregnant. I had been obsessing about kids and a family with Bran, but I didn't think that would be for several years, not now. Not this soon. I wasn't ready. And mostly, I was terrified that whatever ailment I'd just faced would cause me to lose the baby.

I awoke, crying, with the memory of Bran's hand on my stomach and a look of awe on his face. I wanted to hold on to that perfect memory even in my misery. I wanted it to be real and true.

I rolled over and buried my face in his chest. His scent soothed my aching body more than anything else could. I was so weak that the simple motion took nearly all my strength. Bran stirred and he toyed with the ends of my hair, twirling a curl with his fingers.

"You're awake," he said in a husky voice.

"Barely," I replied, finding my throat parched and my voice just a whisper.

He opened his eyes to look at me. "Hey, you're crying. What's wrong? Are you hurting? Are you going to be sick again?"

I shook my head and pain shot through it. I squeezed my eyes shut, overwhelmed by how much it hurt.

"Ruby, I need to know you're okay, sweetheart," he said sternly.

"I-I'm fine," I stuttered softly.

"Would you like to try to sit up and eat something? Maybe even a drink of water?"

I could feel his wolf close to the surface and knew he desperately needed to do something, take care of me or protect me in some way.

"I'll try," I offered, wanting him to calm down.

He eased out from under me and helped me to sit up before he disappeared into the kitchen. A short time later he returned with a bottle of water and a steaming cup. He handed me two aspirins and the water. I gratefully took it. It felt like I was swallowing a rock getting them down, but I managed. I waited with baited breath until those few sips hit my stomach, praying that I wouldn't throw them right back up. After a few minutes I felt like I could relax a little, and was optimistic I wouldn't puke.

"How about some broth? Lily made it last night before she left. She said it should be easy enough on your stomach to keep down. I have a few crackers as well, if you want.

"Okay, let's start with the soup."

The soup didn't feel much better going down than the water and pain meds, but sip by sip I managed it. When I had drank as much as I possibly could, I set the mug down on the nightstand.

"Better?" Bran asked.

I looked at him and nodded, and then burst into tears.

Bran wrapped me in his arms and held me until my tears ran dry.

"Do you want to talk about it?"

I pulled back and looked at him. "I'm so scared, Bran. What if we lose the baby over this? I've never been that sick before."

He stiffened and I could see the worry on his face, too.

"Doc says the baby should be fine, but that it's too early to tell for sure. It's possible it wouldn't even show up on a pregnancy test yet. The only reason they even suspect it is because you weren't able to shift. So we just have to wait and see. Whatever happens, we're in this together."

I nodded and gave him a quick kiss on the cheek. I desperately needed to brush my teeth after everything that had happened. My mouth felt dry and pasty.

"I'm going to drive us both crazy until we know for sure," I confessed.

He chuckled. "I have no doubts about that. Doc said it would be another three to four weeks before we could really be certain. I mean, let's face it, unless the kid's not mine you can't be more than three weeks pregnant, and that would be if we conceived the moment we bonded or in those first few days."

I gave him a stern look. "Of course the kid's yours. Who else's would it be?"

He shrugged. True, I hadn't exactly been a virgin, but I had been on a break from men for a few months before he came into my life.

I laughed. "I'd have to be like four or five months pregnant for it not to be yours, and I think we for sure would have known before now if that were the case."

"Ruby, there's a chance you aren't pregnant, too."

"Then why couldn't I shift, Bran?"

"I don't know, sweetheart. I asked the same thing over and over and no one could come up with a better answer. I just don't want you to get your hopes up too much before we know for sure."

My shoulders slumped. Did that mean he was hoping I wasn't pregnant? Did he not want a baby? We had never really discussed kids beyond that one time, but he had seemed okay with the idea.

Bran smiled and brushed a stray curl behind my ear.

"I don't need a telepathic connection to know exactly what you're thinking. I would be thrilled to find out you are definitely carrying my child. Nothing would make me happier. I know it's all happening fast, but I'm okay with that. I just don't want us to get too excited only to find out it was a fluke."

He leaned in to kiss me, but I pulled back. There was a look of hurt in his eyes.

"Trust me, until I brush my teeth and gargle with the entire bottle of mouthwash, you do not want any part of this," I said, motioning towards my mouth.

He stood, leaned over, and kissed the top of my head instead.

"Let me know when you're ready for that. And don't take too long, because I'd really like to kiss my mate."

I hugged him and let his scent soothe me.

"Okay, let's see if I can stand. You'll probably have to help me to the bathroom."

I leaned on him a lot more than I thought I'd need to. My legs were rubbery and I felt far weaker than I'd imagined. Once at the sink I could lean on it instead, and at least I didn't have to ask Bran to assist with my cleaning up. I vaguely remember him giving me a bath before the world went dark. It was humiliating and pathetic. I would have to work hard to rebuild my strength and if I were with child, that made it even more important for me to be strong enough to protect my baby.

I brushed and gargled about a dozen times. I think I was trying to erase the memories as much as the taste in my mouth. I'd had my fair share of hangovers, but this topped them all.

There was a knock at the door and I saw the panic on Bran's face.

"I'm fine and I promise I won't move until you get back."

"Okay, I'll be quick."

He disappeared and I could hear voices speaking softly, but I couldn't tell who it was until my mother peaked her head into the bathroom.

A tear escaped and ran down my cheek.

"Hi, Mom," I said.

"Oh, my baby girl. I had to see for myself that you were okay. Lily and Thomas filled us in and I waited at their insistence, but a mother should be here to care for her baby. I'm sorry you were so sick."

"I'm okay now, Mom, or I will be at least. Can you call for Bran? I think I need to get back to bed."

Instead she walked to me and wrapped a strong arm around my waist.

"Come on, I've got you."

"I promised him I wouldn't move until he got back."

"He's in there talking to your father and filling him in on how you're doing."

I wanted to be stubborn and wait, but I caved and allowed Mom to help me back into bed.

"Don't hold back on my account, Ruby. How are you holding up?" she asked once I was settled.

"Honestly, I'm not sure yet. My head still feels like it's in a fog and I'm processing everything pretty slowly. Did they tell you I wasn't able to shift?"

She smiled and nodded, brushing some hair back from my face. "Lily told me. Doc thinks you may be pregnant, but that it's still too early to confirm. How are you feeling about that?"

"Terrified," I admitted.

She smiled. "I thought maybe you would be. I mean, Bran disrupted your life pretty good already, and you've never been big on changes, but a baby is a happy occasion, Ruby, and I know you'll make a wonderful mother."

"Mom," I said, rolling my eyes. "I'm not terrified of being pregnant. I'm terrified they were wrong, or that I'll lose the baby because I was so sick. I want children more than anything."

Mom seemed a little surprised at my admission, but she smiled proudly and hugged me. "I have a good feeling everything's going to be just fine," she said.

Bran walked in to check on me, followed by my Dad. Dad turned white at the sight of me.

"Geez, do I really look that bad, Dad?" I teased him.

"Yes," he said honestly. "Are you certain she's okay?" he asked Bran.

"Daddy, I'm right here, and I'm fine," I told him. "Sure I've had better days, but compared to the last few, I'm doing great."

He blanched at the thought and I realized I hadn't really looked at myself in the mirror. I didn't want to see how bad I looked. Judging by my dad's reaction, maybe I should have.

"You still look beautiful to me," Bran reassured me.

"You have to say that unless you plan on sleeping on the couch," I teased him.

He just smiled back, and I could see he was goading me and looked relieved that there was still a spark of sass in me.

"Have you eaten?" Mom asked, changing the subject entirely.

As the former Pack Mother, she had always cared for people. It made her happy and kept her sane in times of crisis. Feeding people was her favorite way to care for them.

"I did. Lily made some chicken broth last night and I was able to hold a little of it down this morning."

"She's on broth and water only for right now. We'll upgrade this evening if she manages to keep that down," Bran said to my mom, before turning to me. "If you'd like more, there's plenty, and don't forget your water bottle is on the nightstand."

Mom reached over and grabbed it, then handed it to me. She gave me an encouraging smile to drink, so I did. It still felt like a large lump in my throat, but I got a few more sips in just to show them I was trying, before putting the cap back on and setting it next to me.

"How about you, Bran? When was the last time you ate?" she asked, turning her attention to my mate.

He shrugged. "I don't know. Lily could probably tell you. Truth be told, the last few days are a bit of a blur for me."

"I imagine so. Your wolf must have been insane," Dad said.

"Helpless is probably the best word for it. Knowing there's nothing I could have done to help her in any way. That was the worst part of it, for me at least."

I reached my hand out and he climbed on the bed next to me to take it.

"But you were helping," I insisted. "You held my hair back. You kept a cooling cloth on my neck and cleaned me up whenever I needed it."

Mom wiped a tear from her eyes and reached over to put her hand over the both of ours.

"Those are the little things that matter most. All we've ever wanted for our children was for them to find someone that made them happy, someone who would stand by their side. And you've proven that these last few days, Bran. I'm so happy you found each other."

Dad walked up and rubbed Mom's shoulders. "She's right. We always knew Ruby would need a strong mate, but one willing to compromise and walk beside her, not in front of her. God knew what he was doing when he paired the two of you."

Bran

Chapter 19

Days later, Zach Collier's words still weighed heavily on me. *God knew what he was doing when he paired the two of you.*

Kelsey and Kyle had returned to Westin with no further altercations from me and the burning in my blood had subsided greatly.

Ruby was still recovering at home without protest. It worried me more than anything. I knew she was worried about the baby, but Doc said she was free to return to work and she had refused, placing herself on bedrest. The way she was protecting our unborn child—or possible unborn child because we didn't even have confirmation that she was indeed pregnant—gave me some relief about their future.

After a full week, she had become restless and irritable, though. She was calling Clay every hour for updates at the dairy. He had been taken out of rotation entirely and assigned to her. I had spoken with the poor guy a few times, but he seemed to be taking it in stride. Turned out it was the job he had always wanted, and he was thrilled with his newfound responsibilities, but he did confess that he didn't think Ruby trusted him to do the job.

"She calls me all the time with reminders of things she thinks I'll forget," he had confided in me. "Simple stuff that anyone should know to even work here."

I had promised to talk to her and get her to back off, and I tried.

"Sweetheart, you either have to get up and go back to work yourself, or you have to leave Clay alone to do things his way."

"His way? There is no his way, Bran," she argued. "That's my responsibility. I worked hard to establish our routine and keep things running smoothly."

"And you trained him well. He knows what he's doing, Ruby. You know he knows exactly what to do, or you would never have trusted him in that position to begin with," I reminded her.

"But the baby, Bran. I can't risk any more than I have already," she admitted.

I kissed her forehead. "Ruby, what's happened has happened. You have to remember, you and I are tough, and our kid is going to be doubly tough. You cannot stay in bed just waiting and hoping things work out for the next nine months. Even Doc says you need to be up and moving. It's not healthy, and I'm worried about you."

She sighed. "I know. I just want everything to work out so badly."

"I know, so do I," I admitted, and the truth of it slapped me in the face. I wanted my mate to carry my child. I wanted a lifetime to love them both and I not only regretted the decisions that led me here, but I hated my Alpha for the position he was holding me in. I was fighting back anger at the events that had happened and the guilt over the role I had played.

"Help me up," she finally said. She was still so weak from the poison that it terrified me. "Okay, I'm out of bed. I still feel terrible and shaky. I can't just go back to work and show this much weakness. We're wolves, they'd know and take over my position."

"No one is after your position. They are all just as worried about you as I am."

"I know, I know. I'll take today and through the weekend to move around and get my energy levels back up, and I'll go back to work on Monday."

"Well, I don't want you rushing yourself either. But getting up and moving is a great first start."

In the beginning, just walking to the bathroom was still tough on her. It was surreal how much a sickness and seven days in bed could weaken a person so quickly. But by Sunday she was eating normally again, and her strength had rebounded quickly. She'd lost too much weight from the sickness and still looked frail to me, but when Lily had come by to check on her for the millionth time, she was thrilled and gushed over how well my mate looked.

Cole and Lizzy were only going to be in town a few more days. The repairs to their house were coming along great and nearing completion; however, we were down one by Gage leaving, as he and Clara had finally gotten the call they had been waiting for, and within an hour they were just gone. I had no idea what it was they did, but they both seemed excited for their new adventure.

I tried to pitch in as much as I could, but most of my focus had been on Ruby, and I knew everyone understood that.

Thomas called me Sunday evening asking if I could come by the Alpha house to see him. When I told Ruby, she asked if she could tag along. It was the first time she'd left the apartment in over a week and I was thrilled for it.

Shelby was there, as well as Ruby's parents, and they doted over my mate from the second we walked into the house. Thomas peaked his head out of his office and motioned me in. When I walked into the room, Cole Anderson was there, too.

I gulped and tried to steady my heartrate. Were they on to me? I had a sinking feeling that was what this was all about. They'd identified the poison and were confronting me about it. I shook hands with Cole, plastered a fake smile on my face, and took a seat next to him.

"What's going on?" I asked, surprised at how normal my voice sounded.

Thomas closed the door then sat across from us. He pulled out his laptop and soon Kyle Westin's face appeared

"Doc ran some tests on the cake the girls ate," Thomas started after we had said our hellos to Kyle. We all went silent and I could feel the sweat dribbling down my back. I started to break out into my confession and beg for forgiveness, but he went on. "This doesn't leave this room. Are we clear?"

Cole looked to Kyle, who nodded his approval. It was one of the rare occasions that I realized Cole's allegiance still resided first and foremost with Westin Pack.

"Agreed," Cole answered for the both of them.

"Of course," I said.

"The girls were poisoned. We're not sure what it was. Doc's checked it thoroughly and says he's never seen the composition of it before. I've gone through the ingredients list that Peyton used, and the substance doesn't match any of them. We've checked the supplies at the diner, and everything looks fine. I think this was definitely done on purpose."

"We suspected as much," Cole said. "The horse that threw Kelsey had already been wiped down and cleared before I was able to get to the stables, but a closer look at the saddle used revealed that there were burrs placed on the underside of the saddle that I believe caused the horse to react like that. I spoke with several of the ranch hands and no one could think of any circumstance where burrs would naturally find their way there. Especially since the horses were carefully brushed down before they were saddled, and no similar incidents have been reported."

"Shit! So it's as we feared, someone's after my mate?" Kyle said, and I could see the anger flaring up in him. I understand that feeling now.

"We can't be certain, but it's a solid theory."

"So what? The other girls were just innocent bystanders?" I asked.

"Yeah, that's what I'm thinking," Cole agreed. "Someone knew that cake was for Kelsey and poisoned it. I don't know when or how, but I'm convinced of it."

A man I didn't know came on the screen next to Kyle.

"I've increased security around Westin. We need a sample of that cake for testing. I have Silas investigating any possible lead he can find to determine what's going on. There's been no obvious movements, though. We're already monitoring Bulgarian activity despite the alliance that was formed, and everything's been quiet."

"Who's Silas?" I couldn't stop myself from asking.

"Silas is head of Westin Force's Bravo team, an elite group that monitors and handles things for Westin Pack," Kyle filled me in.

The man next to him looked curiously at me and something told me I'd just made a grave mistake.

"Who are you?" he asked.

Kyle spoke before I could. "Patrick, this is Bran, Ruby's mate. Bran, this is Patrick, my sister Elise's mate and one of my Betas. Patrick heads up security for Westin Pack."

Patrick O'Connell. Of course I recognized the man now that I wasn't blinded by nerves. Patrick came from the Irish Clan. He was an Alpha's son too, and if he paid too close attention, he was the one person in Westin that just might recognize me.

All the Alpha kids spent summers together away at camp. It helped to establish alliances and friendships across packs from a young age and kept the old treaties strong. Often other high-ranking children would attend, too. Any children Ruby and I had would be eligible simply because their grandfathers on both sides were Alphas. They would be treated no different than any other Alpha kid because of that unique distinction.

Kyle had gone to camp with my brother Nicholai, but I was a few years behind them. Patrick was two years ahead of me, but we had attended together for several years. That was a long time ago and I prayed he didn't put two and two together. I had told Thomas I was from the Indiana Pack and they would be looking there for me, though there were no real records to speak of out of that pack, so it gave me some anonymous safety—unless they followed the connection between the Indiana and Bulgarian Packs.

"Look, we're all here because we all have a vested interest in finding answers. Poison didn't just show up in that cake. Bran, how's Ruby?" Kyle asked.

I sobered and sighed. "She's going to be okay. She's terrified this caused her to lose the baby, and only just left the house today to come here with me. She's put herself on bedrest until we know something for certain, though Doc keeps telling her it isn't necessary."

Kyle growled. "I'm sorry, man. You have as much to be angry about as I do. Did Doc confirm she's pregnant?"

I sighed and shook my head. "No, but my mate does not want to hear that. She will be a fierce and an excellent mother to our pups someday, of that I am certain."

The guys laughed and nodded. Cole put his hand on my shoulder in support. The brotherhood we'd established during our time working on his house together surprised me and left me with yet another thing to feel guilty about. I wasn't just betraying Kyle Westin, I was betraying all of them, and worst, I was betraying my mate.

My hand seared in pain at the mere thought of refusing to proceed. I bit back against the pain and tried not to respond to it. It was a reminder of the life sentence I'd signed before I'd ever even bothered to know these good people.

"We're about done here. I'll be heading home in two days. A piece of the cake has been preserved and I'll be bringing it back for Silas's team to study," Cole said.

"Thanks, man," Kyle said. "They'll be ready and waiting."

Something called Kyle's and Patrick's attention away and they said goodbye as the screen went dark.

"Okay, that's all for now. Nothing said here leaves this room," Thomas told us, and I felt his Alpha powers wash over us to seal his command. "Cole, if there's anything you need help with, just let me know. Bran, Lily would like to come by and see if she can help get Ruby out of the house. So far every time she's tried, she's been told to stay away."

I looked confused. "I swear, I never told her that."

"No, but Ruby did."

I groaned. "I don't know what to do, Thomas."

It wasn't in me to show weakness in this way, but I was truly worried about my mate.

"She won't leave at all?"

"She asked to come with me tonight and is in there talking to her mom and Shelby, I think. This is the first time she's left the house since she got sick."

"That's a start," Thomas said. "Let me text Lily and give her time to get over here before we go." His phone dinged back with a new message immediately. He smiled. "Shelby let her know and they're in the kitchen baking cookies and talking."

I wasn't prepared for the relief that brought me. "Thank you," I said.

We sat around talking like old friends about nothing in particular, just to give the girls some extra time together before adjourning and walking down to the kitchen.

Ruby was at the table eating freshly baked cookies and laughing. My heart lightened at the sound. I looked at Thomas and he smiled and nodded. He couldn't possibly understand what I was going through, with the concern for my mate compacted by the guilt of the role I'd played in it all.

Ruby

Chapter 20

I didn't want to admit it, but I was glad I'd come over to Mom's. I had been wallowing and scared and I needed to snap out of it.

"That's no way to live, Ruby. We're proud wolves. We don't live in fear," Mom had told me.

But I had been living in fear and that wasn't like me. I vowed not to let it consume me.

For the next few weeks I went back to work but allowed Clay to handle most of the day-to-day functions. I spoke with Thomas and got him the promotion and raise he deserved.

Bran continued to work at the ranch, rotating through jobs and making friends everywhere he went. It amazed me just how seamlessly he fit into my life. There hadn't been any mention of trying to go back to his pack and I was secretly optimistic that we would stay in Collier forever. Plus, as we waited for confirmation of my pregnancy, he insisted on tending to my every whim. I gushed to my sisters how I had lucked out and landed the best mate in the world.

Finally, the day came where we would know for certain if we were expecting parents or something was very wrong with my wolf. I had continued to try to call her forth to no avail.

In my heart I already knew, but that didn't stop my nerves. My hands were literally shaking as we walked into the clinic and sat to wait for our turn.

Bran took my hand and squeezed. I calmed a little as we waited. It wasn't long before Doc's nurse was calling us back. She ran through a quick questionnaire, explained the awkward day I was about to have, and handed me a gown with instructions to strip and change into it.

It seemed odd to me that there would even be such a thing. It wasn't like nudity was any big deal amongst shifters, so why follow the archaic human practices? It made me giggle, a sort of nervous hysteria bubbling just under the surface.

"What?' Bran asked. "Everything's going to be okay."

He must have told me that a million times over the last few weeks.

"I know," I said honestly. "I was just wondering why I have to put this ridiculous gown on when it's not like everyone in Collier hasn't seen me naked before."

A low growl rumbled through Bran as Doc walked in. He looked up and grinned.

"Sorry, Doc," Bran mumbled.

"Not a problem, son. I'm used to it. That's why we have the gowns. Not really necessary in a wolf pack, but I find, especially during pregnancies, that the males become more protective and it's just safer for all of us to practice a little modesty," he explained.

Bran and I shared a look that had me laughing again.

"Let's get on with this, shall we? Did my nurse discuss everything with you already?"

"Basically, it's too early for a normal sonogram, so we have to get up close and personal with that magic wand thingy you're about to stick up my hoo-hah," I said, recapping what the nurse had told us.

Bran shook his head and might even have blushed a little, but Doc never missed a beat as he flipped on a monitor then placed my feet in the stirrups, gently nudged my legs apart until they fell slack, and began slathering up the magic wand.

"I'm not sure I've ever heard it described quite so eloquently," Doc said as I tensed from the discomfort of the wand.

Almost immediately, what looked like static on an old TV flashed across the screen. He poked and prodded the wand awkwardly and then stopped and smiled.

I squinted to try to figure out what we were looking at. He pointed to a little dot on the screen, then hit some buttons to zoom in.

"And that's a baby," he finally announced.

I gasped and tears started falling down my cheeks. Bran squatted down close to me and stared in awe, squeezing my hand and kissing my forehead.

"Why does it look like a little tadpole? Where's its legs? Oh my God, what's wrong with our baby?" I asked, starting to freak out.

"Relax Ruby, your pup looks perfect. Right on time for approximately six weeks. Like a tadpole, the legs and other parts will develop over time. I promise you that little one is just fine. Now, let's zoom in a little more and see if we get lucky."

"You can tell what it is already?" I asked.

Doc laughed. "No, not for a few more months." He flicked another switch and turned knob, and a very fast swooshing sound filled the room. "It's really hard to see, but that little flicker and that noise you're hearing is your baby's heartbeat."

"Oh my God," Bran said reverently as I cried a little more.

Too quickly the time passed, the monitor was shut off, and the wand removed. I was still in a daze as I dressed and left the clinic. Once in the truck, Bran and I just sat there staring at each other.

"A baby," I said. "We're really having a baby. I mean, in my heart I knew it, but this just makes it so much more real."

He nodded and hugged me, but not fast enough for me to miss the flash of terror in his eyes. We hadn't planned for this and I'd never even stopped to ask if he wanted this—not that it mattered, because I would do absolutely anything to protect this little pup now, even from its father if it came down to it.

When Bran broke our embrace, I felt no fear in him. He smiled down at me and kissed me. "I know you are going to be an amazing mother." He reached out and placed his hand lovingly over my flat stomach. "Our baby."

I cried a little more, surprised by how emotional I felt. I wasn't much of a crier but this whole experience was overwhelming me, and I knew it was okay to break down in front of my mate. Bran was everything I could have ever hoped for, my perfect mate.

"If someone had told me this was going to happen two months ago, I would have laughed in their face, but I can't imagine any other life or anyone else to go through this craziness with. I love you, Bran."

"I love you, too, sweetheart."

He hugged me again and this time there was a needy feel to it, like he was holding on tightly and would never let go, a promise of our life to come, and I couldn't wait to live it.

There was no sense in trying to keep things secret. There really was no such thing in a wolf pack. So, we headed straight over to the Alpha house. All my family was there and waiting. I didn't have to say a word, as we walked in and cheers went up. According to Thomas, my red nose combined with Bran's perma-grin gave it away before we could make an announcement.

Lily hugged me. "I'm so excited for you. Are you happy?" she asked in a lowered voice.

I looked over at my mate laughing at something my father said. "Very," I confessed.

Shelby walked over to hug me. "Do me a favor and call Maddie first. She still feels like the outsider of the family and blames herself for it, but it would really mean a lot to her."

"I will, tonight. I promise," I said.

I hadn't exactly been "open arms, welcome back," when my youngest sister resurfaced like the ghost of Christmas past. I still didn't really understand her reasonings for being gone for so many years.

Madelyn had disappeared clear off the face of the Earth when she was only sixteen years old. I'd had a front row seat for most of it, and it had been a nightmare for my family. I honestly thought she was dead in a dumpster somewhere, and as we now knew, that was the way her story should have gone.

Instead, a human couple found her and raised her, as well as the child she went on to have as the result of a brutal rape. They really had just left her to die, too. Her son, Oscar, was a sweetheart and probably the biggest reason I softened to her return as quickly as I did.

As luck would have it, Liam, Lily's twin brother, crossed paths with Madelyn and what do you know? He was her one true mate. She was now happily mated and living in Westin Pack with Liam, Oscar, and her new daughter, Sara.

It was still hard for me to fully forgive her for all those years. It wasn't like she was being kept hostage or threatened in any way. Her human family supposedly took great care of her and Oscar and they still remained very close, so I couldn't understand why she'd never picked up the phone at least and called to tell us she was alive and well in all those years.

To each their own, I supposed, and I had mostly forgiven her and accepted her back into the family, but it was still a hard pill to swallow. No matter what happened in my life or how bad things got, I always knew without a doubt my family would love me unconditionally. I think more than anything, I hated that Maddie didn't seem to understand that, too.

Even still, as I promised Shelby, on our drive home I called Maddie.

"Ruby?" she answered. "Ruby, is everything okay?"

"Uh, yeah, why wouldn't it be?" I asked.

I could hear Madelyn let out a sigh of relief. "No, no, of course nothing's wrong. I was being silly, it's just, you never call me. Why are you calling?"

I felt guilty at her admission. It was true. I wouldn't have called her at all if Shelby hadn't asked me to. I would have let Shelbs or Lizzy share my good news with her.

I rolled my eyes, even knowing she couldn't see it. "Nothing bad, I promise. It's just, Bran and I had our sonogram today and I'm having a baby. I just wanted to let you know." It sounded lame even to my own ears, and I was ready to beat Shelby for sticking us into this awkward situation, until Madelyn squealed in my ear.

"Eeek! Shelby had told me it was a possibility, but I'm so excited for you, Ruby. And just think, your pup will grow up with Sara! Oh, I hope it's a girl. We only have boys so far in the family here. Oh, but a son is so special, too. Whatever. I know I'm jumping ahead of myself. I'm just so happy for you, Ruby. You're going to make a wonderful mother. You were always the strongest and fiercest of us all."

I was stunned silent by her ramblings. Me? The strongest? The fiercest? I'd never really considered that. I was the one who had stayed home and kept the safe life. Sure, I held my own with the boys, but that was just stubborn pride. I didn't consider myself strong. I certainly didn't feel it with all these emotions today either.

"Ruby? You there?" Maddie asked.

"Yeah, I'm here. Thanks, Maddie I've seen how awesome your kids have turned out, so that really means a lot to me."

"Hey, what's going on? Are you okay?" I heard Liam asking in the background.

"I'm fine. Ruby called to tell me she's pregnant," my sister told her mate.

"Ruby actually called you? Sweetheart, that's great," he said, and for the first time I realized that maybe the wall I'd kept between my youngest sister and I should be taken down.

I wasn't ready to fully forgive the years she'd left us, but I was happy she was back in our lives and I did love her. Family was everything to me and I made a personal vow to reach out and stop keeping her at arm's length.

"Well, I guess you're going to have to get used to hearing from me now. I mean, who else am I going to ask about this stuff? You're the only one of us who's been through having a baby before," I told her, and I could hear her sniffling and knew she was crying.

Maddie had suffered enough, and I needed to step up and be the big sister and let go of the past once and for all.

"You can call me anytime, day or night. I'm here now," she said softly.

"I have a few other calls I have to make still, but we'll talk soon," I promised before hanging up.

I hadn't realized Bran had parked the truck and we were already home.

"Are you okay?" he asked.

I did a quick internal evaluation. Was I? I smiled over at him. "Yeah, everything's perfect."

Bran
Chapter 21

It had been nearly two full months since we'd confirmed Ruby's pregnancy with my pup. Thomas and I were working with a contractor on plans to expand the tiny apartment I shared with Ruby to accommodate a nursery, because Ruby was adamant that we were not moving. She didn't know it yet, but we were already discussing further expansion and debating between doing it now or later.

It had been Thomas's idea. He said he had never really considered Ruby the maternal type to want a big family, but it was all my mate talked about since the sonogram. I was more than a little overwhelmed. I mean, we didn't even have this pup safely in our arms yet, and she was already talking about the next one. Worse, I didn't know if I'd be around for a "next one." Of course I couldn't mention that part to Thomas, so I just smiled and nodded and told him I was fine with whatever he thought was best.

When I wasn't busy on plans for the apartment or doting over my beautiful mate, I had actual friends I sometimes hung out with. The guys around the ranch were awesome and had accepted me as if I had been born into the pack, and I loved my job. Plus, we were always doing stuff with the Collier family.

I had made my rounds of shadows and was finally taking my own assignments. Thomas talked to me about management positions, but I assured him I was fine where I was for the time being, and with the baby on the way I didn't need that extra pressure.

Life was pretty damn good and for the most part I tried to just enjoy it and forget about the oath I had taken. With Kelsey in

Westin, I didn't feel the call of it as pressing, though the dagger on the top shelf in my closet taunted me regularly.

I hadn't dropped my guard entirely, though. Peyton had persuaded Ruby to continue with their training. Sometimes Shelby even joined them. I was satisfied with the results. I was confident Peyton and Ruby could hold their own against any threat presented to them, and Shelby had nearly caught up, too. I didn't even have to coach them any longer, as the girls encouraged and trained each other.

I lied to myself that this was my new life, and everything was going to work out just fine. Then one day as I was finishing up work and walking in from the fields, my phone rang. I dusted my hand off on my jeans and looked at the screen. It was a strange number I didn't recognize.

"Hello?" I asked after swiping to accept.

"Branimir. So good to hear your voice, my beloved."

I stopped in place, a chill running down my spine. "Alpha," I said softly, unable to believe he'd call and risk everything. I quickly looked around to ensure no one was in the area.

"Don't sound so fearful, Branimir, or, I hear you go by Bran now. Smart move, less foreign sounding. My sources are reporting some very concerning things, Bran. I am not pleased."

"Your sources?" I asked.

My Alpha laughed, causing the hair on my neck to stand up.

"You really didn't think I would leave such an important task solely on your shoulders, did you? I've had people in place there far longer than you. Even before the mating alliances between Collier and Westin I knew the Alphas were close, the young Alphas even closer. This has been planned since the moment we suspected the witch was alive. It's only a matter of time before her life is ended."

His pause made me shiver.

"Now, Bran, I'm hearing some very concerning things coming out of Collier. I must admit, I knew you were dedicated, but never dreamed you'd go so far as to mate one of the Alpha's sisters. That was a bold move, destined to get you in and close to the Westins quickly. But I understand the witch visited and yet she still lives. Can you please explain to me why that is?"

I gulped. How the hell was this information getting back to him? I knew I could no longer trust anyone in Collier outside of my family. My family? I thought for a minute. Ruby was definitely my family, but so were Peyton and Shelby, and Zach and Cora. I gulped again. And Lily and Thomas. I couldn't think straight beyond that. My wolf was feeling protective of all of them. When had they become family to me?

"I tried Alpha, but I was never actually introduced to the witch. I took advantage of several opportunities from afar, but they just weren't enough."

"Yes, yes, so I heard. Even going so far as to poison your own mate. I assume that was you?"

"Yes, sir," I admitted, trying not to sound like I was talking through gritted teeth. "I underestimated the poison's effect, I'm afraid, or perhaps baking it caused a change in the poison's composition. Regardless, it only made the witch sick."

My Alpha laughed and I could hear him clapping. I had to take several deep breaths to keep from growling a warning back at him.

"Ruthless. Sheer ruthless. I knew you were the right man for the job. I have it on good authority that another opportunity for you is about to arise. Be armed and ready for it this time," he said. "We'll talk again soon."

The line went dead, and I squeezed the phone in anger until the screen cracked beneath my hand. I threw it across the field as I screamed out to the universe in frustration.

I bent over, hands on my knees, taking deep breaths to try and calm myself. I hadn't lost control of my wolf in a very long time, but I was close to doing just that.

My phone started ringing, and shaking all over, I forced myself to walk towards it. A fear mixed with anger consumed me at the sound and I knew it probably would from now on. I looked at the screen and my entire body shook, trying to calm down at the sight of Ruby's picture.

"Hello?" I answered.

"Hey hon, I'm going to just place an order at the diner tonight and pick it up on my way home from Mom's in a bit. Is there anything in particular you feel like eating tonight?"

I started to relax a little, and smiled at the sound of her voice.

"I'm not all that hungry, so anything is fine," I assured her. "You know what I like."

"Okay. I should be home in about an hour and I have some exciting news to share. See you in a bit."

She hung up before I could question what she meant. I was grateful for a little time to just relax and calm myself down after the phone call I'd received. I stripped out of my clothes and left them in a pile on the ground, right in the middle of the field. Then I shifted quickly and ran.

I needed to feel the wind through my fur and calm my beating heart, or at least have it racing from sheer adrenaline. I needed to block out everything that had happened. I wanted to drown out the voice of my Alpha and all the questions racing through my head.

I did something I had rarely ever done in my life—I gave myself over to the beast.

I wasn't certain how long I'd been running, but my wolf was loyal to our mate, and when we had circled back and returned to the pile of clothes I'd left behind, he sat and waited until I was ready to return to my skin.

When I did, I dressed and picked up my phone. One hour had passed. I shook my head and smiled. It dawned on me that my wolf needed our mate as much as I did. I jogged the rest of the way back, took the stairs two at a time, and walked into an empty house.

Figuring Ruby was just running behind, I jumped at the chance to grab a shower instead of just sitting around waiting. When I stepped out, she was there waiting for me.

"You have no idea how bad I want to jump you right now, but dinner's getting cold," she said with a sly grin.

I pulled her into my arms and kissed her deeply. We hadn't been having sex as regularly as we had pre-baby news. She had this unfounded fear that we would somehow hurt the baby. When we did it was slow and vanilla, but I could handle that much better than a permanent case of blue balls.

"Maybe the food can just be reheated later," she said in a whisper against my lips.

My stomach chose that moment to growl. I hadn't come in for lunch since I'd been out on the range and I suddenly regretted that decision.

Ruby pulled back and laughed. "Fine. We'll eat," she teased.

I was disappointed, but my stomach was happy to feast on our meal. I could tell she was bubbling with excitement over something as we ate.

"You said you had something to tell me. What's up?" I asked.

"Okay, I was going to wait till dessert, but I'm so excited I have to tell you. You know I've been talking to Madelyn a lot lately and we've sort of reconnected and she's really been helping me through this pregnancy stuff, navigating the hormones, and all that craziness, right?"

"Right," I said, wondering where she was going with all this.

"Well, turns out Thomas needs a run to Westin and since I've been wanting to get out there and visit Maddie anyway, he's letting us tag along! Don't worry, it's strictly vacation for us, but I can't wait to introduce you to her. Cole and Lizzy will be there, and of course you already know Kyle and Kelsey, too. Anyway, we leave in the morning. I already packed for us."

She continued to ramble on, but I just sat there in shock. *Another opportunity for you is about to arise.* My Alpha's words were stuck on repeat in my head. How did he know?

* * * * *

The next morning, we were up bright and early. Good to her word, Ruby had us packed and the bags waiting at the front door. She must have been up early because she made breakfast burritos for us to grab and go.

I had barely slept a wink. I was exhausted, grumpy, and terrified. Maybe I was imagining the throbbing of my hand all night, I wasn't even certain. What I did know was that the perfect life I had mustered here in Collier was coming to a crashing end today. There was no way the blood oath would allow me to leave Westin Pack territory with Kelsey alive. Either she died or I died. There was no alternative, and as I stepped on the plane a short time later, there was no going back.

Ruby

Chapter 22

As I sat on the plane next to Bran, I could hardly contain my excitement. San Marco was a beautiful town, so different from Collier. Maddie and I had been talking several times a week and it surprised me how badly I wanted to see my baby sister.

Bran kept looking over at me and shaking his head with a smile on his face. I think my excitement was evident.

He hadn't seemed as thrilled about the surprise trip as I'd hoped. He had friends in Westin. Cole and Kyle would be there. Plus Wyatt, Austin, and Conlin were all joining us, and he was good friends with each of them.

Sometimes it was like there was this darkness deep inside him. I only ever saw glimpses of it, and had never asked. Depression maybe? I had no idea and he certainly went out of his way to try and hide it or battle it down, perhaps. He had never given me any reason to worry, but there was a certain melancholy surrounding him now that scared me.

Maybe he was just a creature of habit, like me. I wasn't a big fan of things like this being sprung on me at the last minute either. It was hard to say, but I felt this wall up between us that I hadn't been able to breech all morning. It was like he was here and by outward appearances he was his normal happy self, but I could feel something wasn't quite right between us.

I bounced in my seat as I looked out the window, part in excitement, part in nerves.

Bran nudged me and smiled, though it didn't quite reach his eyes. "Would you settle down. We still have an hour to go. You're really excited about seeing Maddie, aren't you?"

It was the most he'd said all day and I relaxed, wondering, not for the first time, if I was just worrying too much and seeing something that wasn't there.

"Don't make fun," I teased back. "I am excited. And you get to meet the rest of my family, too."

"Hey, speaking of which, Gage called yesterday. They're coming home today. He asked me to go over this morning and air out the house and pick up a few things before they got there."

"What? Why didn't you say so? We could have done that before we left this morning."

I shrugged. "It was an early morning. Stop worrying. Thomas is taking care of it. I called him after you passed out last night."

"I hope they're home still when we get back. I've missed Clara. They've been gone longer than usual this time."

"Gage said they'd worked four back-to-back jobs and should be home at least a month, so you'll get plenty of time to catch up with Clara."

I sat back in my seat and linked my arm with his as I leaned in and rested my head on his shoulder. "I love that he called you. I love that you fit in so well with my family."

He turned and kissed the top of my head as I closed my eyes.

The early morning must have been weighing heavily on me, because my eyes refused to open again as the adrenaline fled my body and I was suddenly very tired.

I could hear Bran talking and laughing with the other men as I slowly drifted off to sleep.

"Sweetheart, wake up. We're here," Bran said as he gently shook me.

"Already?" I asked as I yawned and stretched.

"Hmm, keep that up, and we aren't leaving this plane," he threatened in a deep, sexy voice.

I slowly opened my eyes and beamed up at my mate. His lips crashed down on mine in a possessive, all-consuming kiss. I pulled back and sighed.

"Come on, we should go," I said.

"We don't have to. We could just stay right here, Head back home. No one is expecting us back for four whole days. We wouldn't even have to leave the bed."

"That does sound glorious, but since we're here, let's go."

There was a hesitation. I was certain I felt it this time, but he recovered quickly and nodded with a solemn look on his face. I couldn't fathom what was going on or why he was acting so weird, but I knew something was bothering him.

Our suitcases were already waiting on the tarmac, so I grabbed his hand and we rose to exit the plane. Also, there was a car already waiting for us, and the second my feet hit the pavement I was tackled with little arms wrapping around my waist.

"Aunt Ruby! You're here," Oscar exclaimed with excitement.

I looked around until I saw Maddie and Liam standing off to the side. She passed the baby to her mate and started walking towards us. She looked strong and confident, not like the girl that had arrived in Collier last year with a family of her own and a bit sheltered by Lily and Liam.

I met her halfway and hugged my sister tightly.

"You look so good, Maddie," I gushed.

"Me? Look at you. You're practically beaming."

After we'd learned everything Maddie had been through, I'd looked at her as a victim. I had been wrong. This beautiful, strong, confident woman before me wasn't a victim, she was a survivor. It was probably there before, I'd just been too stubborn, too hurt, too pigheaded to notice. I would be forever grateful to my pup for giving me back Maddie, and to Shelby for pushing me to make that call, though I would never in a million years admit that to Shelbs.

"Come on, Liam has the car waiting," she said, as she led us away from the waiting SUV.

Bran and I shared a look in confusion as Wyatt waved, and then shut the door to the SUV just before it took off.

"Uh, guess that wasn't for us," I mumbled.

Maddie laughed. "Of course not. Patrick runs things a bit like a military base at times with new people. They will be taken straight to headquarters and cleared before they let them head into town. You guys are family. There's no need for all of that."

"That's crazy," I said. "I thought y'all got a lot of tourists and such up this way. How does he stop that?"

"Oh, he doesn't," Liam said as he took the suitcases from Bran, then shook his hand with a nod. "He just does the best he can. They monitor new cars by license plates and facial recognition to watch for anything concerning, but they don't actually stop and check or interrogate people. It's all done very low-key. Still, this is different, because they're visiting shifters, here for the first time."

"They've never visited here before?" Bran asked.

"It's not normal for wolf shifters to enter another Pack's territory, Bran," Liam went on. "We have a certain leniency between Collier and Westin just because of our families. I mean, with Maddie and Lizzy mating into Westin, and Lily mating into Collier, it's brought the two packs uniquely close, but even still, it's only higher ranked pack members or family that typically cross the pack lines."

"So why are they here? It was never said," Bran asked.

"Thomas sent them to help out on some project or another," I said. "Kyle needed a few extra hands. I tuned out the why and was just excited that it meant we could tag along."

"I can't believe you're actually here!" Maddie squealed, turning to give me one more hug after clicking Sara into her car seat. "And Bran, it's really great to finally meet you," she said to my mate.

"I'm so sorry. I didn't even make introductions. Bran, this is my baby sister, Maddie, her mate Liam, and their precious kids, Oscar, and little Sara." I gushed at the baby, who had grown so much since the tiny little thing she'd been the last time I saw her.

Oscar jumped into the third bench. Bran and I walked around and slid in next to Sara while Liam drove us back to their house. Maddie had a full lunch buffet waiting for us when we arrived. Since Bran and I hadn't eaten breakfast before we left, I realized I was suddenly starving.

"This looks amazing. I am so hungry," I admitted.

I made myself a sandwich to eat while Maddie gave me the tour. Her house was beautiful, nestled in the woods with a gorgeous backyard for the kids. I thought about our place and what it would be like to have kids there. Sure, the woods and the creek with the playset out back were great, but my pup had an entire barnyard and miles and miles of open space in his or her backyard. What kid wouldn't love that?

We spent the day at Maddie and Liam's, just hanging out, getting to know each other, playing with the kids, and eating.

I was in my second trimester now and felt like I was always starving. I couldn't seem to possibly eat enough. Maddie kept assuring me it was completely normal and to just enjoy it and eat.

While sitting around the back deck talking after the kids went to bed, Maddie's cell phone rang.

"It's Elise. I should grab this," Maddie said. "Hello? What? How did that happen? Okay, yeah, we're on our way now," she said, hanging up the phone.

"That was Elise. Kelsey's been in an accident. It's bad. We need to go now. Micah's at home with her. He's our Pack physician. Come on." She grabbed my hand as we started to head for the door, then stopped when she realized the kids were already in bed.

"Go," Liam said. "Bran and I will hang back and watch the kids. Just keep us posted. I'll wake them and take them to Mom's if need be, but I know you won't rest until you know Kelsey is okay."

I looked to Bran and he nodded in agreement. I gave him a quick kiss on the lips and Maddie and I were off.

It wasn't a long ride to Kelsey's place but both of us were on edge the entire time. I tried to press Maddie for more details, but she just didn't have any. Kelsey had been in a car accident, that was all we knew for certain.

We weren't the only ones to fill the house and check on her, either. The youngest Westin, Chase, and his mate Jenna had recently moved back home to San Marco. They met us at the door.

"How is she?" Maddie asked.

"We don't know much. Micah's still in there with her. Zander woke up from all the commotion, and is scared. Kyle doesn't need to worry about the boys too, so Jenna and I are taking them over to Mom's for the night. We'll hang out there and watch the kids. If Liam needs to drop off Oscar and Sara too, that's fine. We'll just make it a slumber party," Chase said.

Maddie gave him a quick hug. "Thank you. Liam and Bran stayed home with the kids until we find out what all's happening."

"Seriously, it's okay if he wants to leave them at Mary's. Chase and I will watch them. It gives us something to do at least besides just sitting around waiting."

Maddie nodded at her in thanks. "Oh, I don't think you guys have met yet. Jenna, Chase, this is my sister Ruby."

"Hi," Jenna said. "Sorry about all the chaos."

Elise walked over to greet us. "Ruby, I didn't know you were in town. I wouldn't have bothered Maddie with this if I had. I'm so sorry."

"Kelsey's my friend, of course I want to be here too," I told her. "And we just got in this morning. It was a last minute decision. I barely gave Maddie notice."

"Well come on in, find a seat wherever. We're just hanging out and waiting to hear how she's doing."

Chase and Jenna left with Kelsey's sons, and the rest of us settled down for a long night catching up, because in truth there really wasn't anything we could do.

It was hours later before Kyle finally came out of the bedroom. He looked terrible as he stood in the entryway, taking in the room. There had been many more to come and go throughout the night, but now it was just down to me, Maddie, Elise, and Patrick.

"How is she?" Elise asked.

Kyle let out a deep breath and sat down hard on the chair across from me.

"She's going to be okay. I had to use my Alpha powers to force her to shift. I could feel how much it hurt her, but Micah felt it was the safest and fastest way for her to heal. He worked as fast as he could to set the broken bones in her wolf form. He only had to re-break two of them. She's physically healing fast, though she's been ordered to stay in wolf form for the next twenty-four hours."

"Bet that pissed her off," Elise commented.

Kyle smiled and nodded. "She's of course more worried about me and the boys than herself."

"That sounds about right," Maddie said.

"Patrick, what happened?" Kyle finally asked.

All eyes turned to Patrick. He was the last one to arrive and had stayed mostly quiet while we girls talked.

Patrick took a deep breath. "This is what we know. She came by the lodge today expecting to meet up with Ruby."

"I guess she didn't know Liam and I picked her and Bran up and went straight back to our place," Maddie said.

Patrick nodded. "She stuck around for a little while, then left. She lost control of the vehicle coming down a hill, she swerved, hit a tree at an odd angle that caused it to roll down a cliff, and stop upside down in the ravine just outside of town."

"I could gather that much, but what happened?" Kyle asked again.

Patrick looked at him solemnly. "Her brake line and power steering were cut at the lodge, Kyle. Cole found the leaks it caused in the parking lot and Archie confirmed the fluids. I physically verified that on the vehicle, or what's left of it as well."

"Oh my God, someone did this on purpose?" Maddie asked.

My little sister began to cry as I wrapped her into my arms for comfort.

"Where were the Collier guests?" Kyle asked through gritted teeth. His wolf was very near the surface and the power he was emitting was terrifying.

"They all checked out, Kyle. Ruby and Bran were the only two that didn't go through processing," Patrick said as all eyes turned to me.

"Don't look at me. We were with Maddie and Liam all day long," I said.

"I know that," Kyle said. "There's no way the two of you could be responsible for this."

"You asked about my Pack though. Is it because of the incidents that happened when you were visiting? Is someone trying to hurt Kelsey?" I asked.

"It's been a concern for sure," Patrick said.

"What?" Elise said. "What happened in Collier and why am I just hearing about this? Oh wait, are we talking about the food poisoning that made Ruby so sick?"

"Amongst other things," her mate said hesitantly.

"Other things?" she asked in that tone that dared him to even hesitate in explaining further.

"It's possible the other was a completely unrelated issue," Kyle said.

"When she was thrown from the horse," I said softly, starting to piece things together.

Kyle nodded.

"Has there been anything strange that's happened to her here, before today?" I asked, not certain I wanted to know the answer to my question.

Patrick shook his head. "Not that we're aware of. There's been a few anonymous threats, but she's a Pack Mother, and that sadly happens all the time to people in positions of authority. We check each and every one out, but have found no true validity behind them."

"So Collier's the link, and there's no way you can dismiss this one. Someone tried to kill Kelsey," I said.

Bran

Chapter 23

Ruby woke me when she climbed into bed and snuggled into my side.

"Is Kelsey okay?" I asked, unsure if I was hoping she'd say yes or no. If Kelsey died and it wasn't my fault, the curse on me would be over and I'd be free to live my life. Liam had been kept informed throughout the night and I knew they were trying to put a case together with very little to go on. Something told me I knew the answers to their questions, I just didn't know who the spy was here in San Marco, or how my Alpha had managed to infiltrate Westin Pack.

"I wasn't able to see her. Kyle has her locked down pretty tightly and Patrick has security monitoring their place. They think someone tampered with her car. Apparently, she's in really bad shape and Kyle used Alpha powers to force her to take wolf form. It's bad, Bran. I'm scared for her."

Guilt and relief simultaneously filled me. I pulled Ruby closer to me and kissed the top of her head. A part of me hoped Kelsey survived this, but a part of me really hoped she didn't. I liked Kyle, and I would miss him if they died, but selfishly I'd choose my mate over his any day and I wanted—no I needed—more time with Ruby.

Ruby was exhausted from the stress of the evening and quickly fell asleep in my arms. I lay awake into the early morning hours going through all the various scenarios. Alpha had said he had others in Collier. He hadn't mentioned any about spies in Westin, and why would they wait until today to act if they had that kind of access to Kelsey?

I thought through the people we'd brought with us. Me, Ruby, Wyatt, Austin, and Conlin. It didn't make any sense. I would vouch for any one of them.

And they would vouch for you too, my inner conscience reminded me.

I needed background checks on all three of them, but I wasn't sure how to go about it without giving myself away. It was too big of a risk.

While Ruby had been gone, I had gotten to know Liam Westin quite well, and damned, if I didn't respect him, too. It was hard to imagine anyone hating the Westins, and yet I did. I had hated them for a very long time without even knowing them. And there were others like me out there. My Alpha had confessed that. That meant if I didn't play my part right, there'd be a target on my head next.

As I laid there, I noticed a strange glow emanating from my bag in the corner. It wasn't much brighter than a cell phone light. I found myself fixating on it until curiosity finally got the best of me and I got up to investigate it, careful not to wake Ruby.

I unzipped the front pocket the rest of the way and stumbled backwards as I dropped to my knees. Inside was the dagger that carried my blood oath. I took it out and examined it closely. The faint glow was coming off my blood as if it were calling to me.

Sharp pain ripped through my hand. The dagger fell to the ground and clinked across the hardwood floor, loud enough to wake my mate.

Ruby peered down from the bed above.

"It's glowing," she said in a sleepy voice. I wasn't one hundred percent certain she was even fully awake yet. "It's beautiful."

"Sweetheart, why was this in my bag?"

"It's your dagger," she said, as if that was explanation enough.

"Yes, but it usually stays . . ."

"On the top shelf of your closet," she interrupted to finish for me.

"Right," I said.

She frowned. "Wyatt said you needed it and I should pack it for the trip."

"Wyatt?" I asked, certain I had heard her wrong.

"Yes. Wyatt told me where to find it and that it was important to bring along."

"You're positive it was Wyatt?" I asked.

"Yes, he stopped by the apartment yesterday to tell me. What's going on, Bran?"

I could tell she was starting to fully wake, so I picked up the dagger and shoved it back into the bag, zipped it closed, and climbed back into bed with her.

"Is everything okay?" she asked.

I kissed the top of her head, sliding back into my position as her personal body pillow, and assured her everything was just fine. She sighed and drifted back to sleep.

Wyatt? He was my friend. My first real friend in Collier. I should have known better, yet I still had a hard time believing it. Wyatt? It just didn't make sense. Maybe the Alpha was threatening his mate. That was the only reason I could think of for someone like Wyatt to get involved in this kind of mess.

I never fully slept as plans and ideas kept playing out in my head. I needed to act quickly. The moment the sun rose, I was out of bed and hitting the shower.

I guess I had Sara to thank for the fact that Liam was up early and already had coffee brewing. I was going to need a lot of it to get through the day.

The baby sat cooing in her high chair, playing with a pile of dry Cheerios while Liam sat next to her eating a bowl himself.

"Cereal?" he asked, nodding towards the kitchen counter for a full selection.

"Sure, thanks," I said, finding what I needed and settling down at the table across from him.

"Ruby fill you in on what happened?" he asked.

"Yeah, for the most part. It's crazy, right?"

"Patrick's over at Kyle's going through a few things. Thought I'd give him a fresh set of eyes. Want to tag along?" he asked.

The blood in my veins started to boil and I knew this was it. I solemnly agreed.

After dinner, he cleaned up Sara and grabbed a bag of her things. We dropped her off at the Alpha house with his parents before driving over to the cabin where Kyle and Kelsey preferred to live.

As we pulled up, I saw Wyatt hanging around outside and unease set in. I held back.

"You coming?" Liam asked.

"Be there in a minute," I said, walking straight for Wyatt. "Hey Wyatt, what are you doing here?"

He shrugged. "Don't rightly know. Patrick O'Connell called us all in first thing this morning for interrogations. Austin just came out and Conlin's in there now. I think they believe one of us was somehow involved in Kelsey's accident yesterday. It's crazy."

I let that drop for a moment. There was something more pressing I needed first.

"Hey, did you tell Ruby to pack my dagger for this trip?"

"Well, yeah. I told her the correct one, right?" he asked.

My blood continued to boil being this close to the witch, but also in a far more personal way as betrayal set in.

"How'd you know about that, Wyatt?" I asked.

Wyatt had been my first friend. I trusted the man even in a world where I knew I couldn't afford to trust anyone. Maybe I should feel relieved that he had my back, that he was on my team, but I didn't. I was disappointed and angry at him.

Wyatt scrunched up his face in frustration. "Look, I was only trying to help. Conlin told me you needed it for the trip and had forgotten to pack it. He told me what it looked like and where to find it and asked if I could remind Ruby to bring it. Sorry if it was a misunderstanding. I was only trying to help a friend," he said in earnest.

"Conlin?" I asked.

"Yeah. He said you asked him to do it, but something came up and he didn't have time to stop by your apartment, so I did it for him."

Part of me breathed a sigh of relief. Wyatt might still be the stand-up guy I had come to know.

"Wyatt, you and Conlin, you're close, right? You guys grew up together, that Six Pack stuff and all, right?" I asked.

"Conlin? Nah. Austin, sure, but not Conlin. He strolled into town looking for work about two or so years ago. I mean, yeah, we're tight, but not like Six Pack tight or anything."

I clapped my hand on his back and thanked him. Conlin walked out of the house and moved to speak with Austin in the opposite direction, though his eyes watched me. I nodded in his direction and let myself into the house.

The pain subsided for a moment, before increasing even worse than before. I was so close. All I had to do was walk into the next room and kill the witch and all the pain would end. There were only two people standing between me and that goal and I knew I could take them both easily.

As I turned in her direction, something caught my eye and distracted me. Patrick had a bunch of pictures spread out across the table. There were some from the scene of the crash, the stains where the lines were cut, and pictures of possible suspects. Mine wasn't even amongst them.

"It has to be Wyatt," Patrick said.

"I just have a hard time believing that. Wyatt is part of Thomas's inner circle. He's like a brother to him, Patrick. It doesn't make sense. What's his motive?"

"I don't know, but he's the only one of the three that had opportunity."

"Walk me through the timeline again," Liam suggested.

"We finished up processing and Wyatt excused himself to use the bathroom. He was gone for over half an hour. Cameras picked him up in the wrong part of the building. He says he got lost trying to find his way back. Austin never left the holding room, and Conlin only did for long enough to walk outside and call for Wyatt. The cameras are on him for all but about five minutes. It's too short a window, but we lost Wyatt on the cameras for over twenty minutes. I don't know how he did it, but it had to be Wyatt."

My phone rang and I looked down to see a strange number similar to the one my Alpha had previously used. I froze. I didn't want to answer it. Why would he be calling right now?

"What do you think of this, Bran? I mean, you know them better than we do," Liam said.

I held up my still-ringing phone. "Give me a minute," I said, walking back outside.

"Is the witch dead?" Alpha's voice made me want to throw up.

"Not yet," I admitted.

I heard him punch something. "Why not? I've made sure you have every opportunity possible, Branimir. You have the knife. I've weakened the girl. You have the access no one else has to her. Just walk in there and put the knife through her heart and all this will end."

I gulped. He had orchestrated it all. I could feel Conlin still watching me from afar. I nodded and showed no external emotions, all while raging inside at being a pawn to his games.

"They still have her locked away with security guarding the door. Only Kyle goes in and out, not even family yet."

"That's because you didn't act fast enough last night. Why were you not by your poor mate's side comforting her last night while their defenses were at their lowest?" There was an eerie pause, followed by a laugh that caused the hair on my arms to stand up. "Of course. You're torn over your mate. I should have predicted this. My beloved, there is no need to fear. I give you my full assurance that in your death, I will claim your mate and unborn child. They will come home and be welcomed by all our pack. Your pup will be raised the son of a victor, not that of a traitor. They will both know what you have done for us and your name shall be revered and celebrated for generations to come. Now finish it."

My entire body was shaking violently, and my wolf was threatening to take control, not to kill Kelsey, but to protect Ruby. I took several calming breaths and managed to say in a clear voice, "Yes Alpha," before the line went dead.

I walked around the side of the house, out of the prying eyes of Conlin, and dialed Thomas Collier's number.

"Hey, Bran. How's it going down there?" he asked.

"Listen close, I only have a minute. You need to call Kyle, give him whatever excuse necessary, send a goddamn plane and get me and Ruby out of here now. I can't stop the chain of events in play if you don't and I can't explain anything over the phone. Now Thomas. I don't have much longer."

I hung up the phone, shoved it in my pocket, and walked back around and inside the house. The pull to Kelsey was stronger than ever. This was the end and I was about to do something that would not only ruin my life, but that of Ruby and our child. too.

Patrick and Liam were still pouring over the details from the couch. Kyle was standing in the corner of the room. His phone rang as I walked in and I almost sighed in relief. Thomas was my only hope now.

"So, Wyatt," Liam said, sounding like Patrick had finally convinced him.

Before I could speak, Kyle hung up the phone and walked over to me.

"Thomas called. There's an emergency back home and he needs you and Ruby to return immediately. I've placed a few quick calls and arranged for one of my planes to be gassed and ready and Cole's picking up Ruby now and will swing by to get you in a few minutes. I really hope everything's okay, and I'm sorry this trip has been so chaotic."

I nodded. "I hope Kelsey makes a full recovery," I said honestly, fighting back the urge to push him out of the way and run down the hall to kill her where she lay.

Kyle was called away, and I turned to walk back outside.

"So what's next?" Liam asked. "I mean, Thomas isn't going to be happy about this. If we're wrong, we could start an inter-pack shitstorm, that I really don't want any part of.'

"Feck, I know," Patrick said, struggling with his decision.

Through the window I saw Cole pull up. I pulled up Notes on my phone and started typing, then walked over to Patrick and Liam. Without a word, I turned Wyatt's and Austin's cards over, and pointed to Conlin. Then I flashed them my phone.

Check again. Run background with facial recognition. Bulgarian spy, the note read.

I pointed to my ears and placed a finger over my lips to let them know he was listening. Before they could even recover, I was gone.

My phone was ringing as I boarded the plane. It was local and I suspected Patrick, but I ignored it.

Ruby was in a huff, frustrated by the barbaric actions of her brother, as she kept reminding me. I stayed quiet, calculating what needed to be done.

Thomas was waiting for us at the airport when we arrived. I gave Ruby the front seat and we listened to her fuss the entire way back to the apartment. Thomas kept giving me questioning looks in the rearview mirror, but for his part he made no excuses or apologies to his sister. Ruby stomped upstairs and slammed the door. I followed with our bags, dropped them off in the living room, and without a word to Ruby, I opened the side window and jumped back down to the ground below.

Thomas was standing by the car and startled. "Jesus, Bran, what the hell?" he asked, looking from me and back up to the windows.

I typed out on my phone *Cameras*, showed him, and after carefully checking my surroundings I slid into the backseat again and laid down on the floorboard.

"This is crazy, you know?" he said as he drove off. "Where are we going?"

"Somewhere we can talk, privately. No chance of others hearing," I said in a low voice.

"I have a dampener in my office."

"Too public. We need private for this," I said again.

"Fine," he said. "I have one at the house, too. Is that okay?"

"Yeah, that should do," I confirmed.

He drove quickly to his house. I hesitated as I checked the surroundings before hurrying inside. I didn't say another word until we were inside his office there and I knew the dampener was on.

"Now what is all this about, Bran? You're acting crazy," Thomas said.

I dropped to my knees before him. "You're not going to like what I'm about to say. You're going to want to banish me, but I'm begging you not to do that, Thomas. Instead, I need you to accept me into your Pack. I will transfer my full allegiance to you, but you have to swear to me that you will take care of Ruby and the baby she's carrying. Promise me, Thomas."

I was desperate and had no other options. He would come for them upon my death and no matter what happened I couldn't allow that. They would be safer here in Collier. I could move on and do what had to be done, but not until I knew they were safe.

"Bran, get up," he said.

I shook my head and refused. I sat back on my feet and my shoulders sagged. "Promise me, Thomas."

He ran a hand through his short hair. "What's all this about?"

"Promise me," I begged again.

Never in my life did I imagine myself on my knees begging for anything, but here I was, broken and desperate.

"Okay, okay. She's my sister. Of course I'm going to protect her and the child," he finally conceded, and the relief I felt was overwhelming.

"Accept me into your pack," I told him. "I give my full allegiance to you on the promise you will take care of my family when I'm not here to do it myself."

I turned my head and exposed my neck to him. He mumbled some words and told me to get up. I didn't feel any different. I worried that it didn't take because of my desperation, but as long as Thomas swore he would protect them, I could die in peace.

I managed to pull myself up into a chair and he sat just across from me. I could feel his desire to speed things up and understand what was happening. I'd largely left him in the dark, but he patiently waited for me.

"I'm not who you think I am," I finally confessed. He didn't react to that, so I went on. "I was sent here by my Alpha to get close to you. Close enough to gain access to the Westins, or specifically Elena, the witch. I was sent here to kill her." Still there was no reaction from Thomas. "I swear to you, I never intended to use Ruby to gain that access. I prepared for every possible scenario, but her. She's my one true mate and I love her more than anything. When my Alpha called today and praised me in advance for finishing the witch, he promised to come for Ruby upon my death, and raved over how they would both be celebrated by my heroism and I dunno, something inside me just snapped. Carrying the burden of a traitor won't be easy for them, but with you and the family surrounding them with love, I know they'll be okay and go on to live a good life. I don't want him anywhere near her or our pup. Do you understand?"

Thomas took a deep breath. He was too calm. I'd just confessed things that should have pissed him off, but he didn't even seem fazed. He leaned back towards his desk and grabbed a folder with my name on it. He tossed it to me.

I opened it slowly. Inside were pictures and notes, accurate ones, about me. He'd known all along.

"Why did you let me stay then? If you knew. Why?"

Thomas sighed. "You were already mated to my sister when we first met. I didn't have time to run a background check, and I was more than a little pissed off about it, if you remember. Collier Pack is a farming town. We run a successful ranch, but I don't hold the resources Kyle does over at Westin Pack. Now he has good reasons for that, you being one of them, but with the alliance we have, I do get full use of those resources when needed."

"You had him run a full background check on me."

"Yeah. I reached out to Patrick pretty much the second you arrived. It took a few weeks to capture a picture he could run facial recognition on, but we already suspected something was up by then. When Kelsey first got hurt here, you were our prime suspect. Confirmation of who you really were came in around the same time. Patrick wanted to pull you out immediately, but I asked him to wait."

"Why?" I asked.

"Why? Because my sister was in love with you by then, and you were pretty convincingly in love with her, too. When the poisoning incident occurred, I couldn't believe it was you. We couldn't pin it to you. I told Patrick there was no way you could knowingly harm your mate like that, and he agreed to keep our suspicions quiet."

"Wait, you mean no one else knows?"

Thomas shook his head.

"Not even Kyle?"

He smiled. "Patrick runs a tight ship on security over there. He also oversees Westin Force, an elite group of operatives that work for them. His reach and resources would blow your mind. He's also a firm believer in the 'need to know' rule, and will be the first to admit that there's a lot of things that Kyle doesn't need to know, including this. He's Alpha, but he's also a mate. Knowing about you would have only distracted him at a time when he's been actively working hard to strengthen a peace agreement, with Bulgaria of all packs."

"My brother is a good Alpha, Thomas. He is not my Alpha," I said.

Thomas scrunched up his forehead and realized I was finally telling him something he didn't already know.

"Nicholai was not behind these attacks?"

"No," I said honestly. "Nicholai is serious about the alliance. Meeting Kyle and Kelsey in person changed him. He came back resolved not to press for revenge of our parents' deaths. You can trust him in the treaty. He has a good heart. I didn't understand it at the time. I was filled with anger and only wanted the revenge I felt we deserved. I gave my allegiance to another."

I pulled out the dagger and handed it to him. Even in daylight there was a faint glow to it. Thomas examined the knife closely and sucked in a deep breath at the realization of what he was looking at.

"I sealed my fate before I ever met her, before I ever stepped foot onto Collier territory, and before I even took time to know the Westins. That's my death certificate. It's a blood oath, forged by a powerful witch. There's nothing I can do to break it, aside from Kelsey Westin's death. The pain when I am near her is excruciating. Its power is strong, and I cannot escape it. All I can do is pray you will keep our deal and protect the woman I love when I am gone."

"Dammit, Bran. This is going to kill her when she finds out."

I knew we were talking about my mate and not the witch I was bound to kill.

"It won't. She's stronger than that, and she'll have our child to protect. She's going to be a fierce and loving mother. I'm so proud of her. It gives me peace."

"The poisoned cake. Was that you?"

I nodded. I crossed my leg over my knee and showed him the hidden compartment in my boot. I pulled out one of the vials and passed it to him. "There is an antidote, but unfortunately I did not bring it with me. These are undetectable by smell or taste. They are designed to pour into a cup of tea, and it's death within the hour. I knew the cake was for Kelsey. When opportunities arrive, the blood oath calls with a persistence you cannot turn away from. I didn't want to do it, but I couldn't bear the pain of ignoring the call. I poured three of those into the batter when Peyton and Ruby left me alone in the room for only a moment. I had no idea how many I needed or what baking would do to the composition of the poison, but it was something, and enough to tamper down the pain. It never even crossed my mind that the other girls would eat it with her."

"Damn. Can't even imagine the guilt of that when you came home to find Ruby so sick."

"It wasn't the first time I regretted the decisions that led me here, but it was the first time I despised myself for them."

"I knew it wasn't on purpose. I don't think for one second you would ever purposefully hurt my sister."

"And yet I am," I said, letting that reality sink in between us. It wasn't a direct attack, but my actions would continue to hurt her, even after my death.

Ruby
Chapter 24

I was pissed when I got back to the apartment. Kelsey was hurt, I should have been there to help out, but Thomas had pulled rank and called us home. Worse, he didn't even bother to explain why.

Bran had been acting strangely, too. He was quiet on the flight back, like he was lost in his own thoughts that I wasn't privy to. I hated when he got that way and after I'd stomped upstairs in frustration and a desperate urge to use the bathroom, I'd walked out to find him gone. The window was open, and our bags were there, but no sign of my mate. Just great.

I'd been stewing over it all afternoon, quite literally as I sat in the kitchen cooking everything I possibly could with the ingredients on hand, and I didn't even know why I was doing that. Stupid pregnancy hormones.

I heard the door open and I felt his presence. It made me madder with the comfort that it brought me. Bran was home. I knew we needed to talk, but mostly I just needed him.

"Hey," he said as he walked into the kitchen. "Wow, something smells incredible."

I sniffed and wiped at my eyes. I didn't want him to know his words of praise affected me even in my darkest funk. Stupid, stupid hormones.

"Where have you been?" I asked without even turning to look at him.

I felt his arms wrap around my waist and his hand rubbed my belly. That small motion made me feel more loved and cherished than I ever imagined possible. He kissed the bond mark on my neck.

"I'm sorry. Thomas and I had some things to discuss," he said.

"And you couldn't even tell me you were leaving?"

"It was urgent, and you seemed kind of pissed off. I thought it was best to just leave."

I turned in his arms and glared at him. "It's never best to just leave."

He gave me a sad smile. I could see there was a lot weighing on him, but I sensed he didn't want to, or simply wouldn't, talk about it.

"I'll remember that for next time," he said as he gave me a quick peck on my nose.

I scrunched it up. "Maybe don't let there be a next time then," I grumbled.

"I'll try to remember that."

His lips slowly brushed against mine. They were soft and hesitant at first, but soon became insistent. I played coy as his tongue persisted, seeking entry. He nibbled on my lower lip and it elicited an unexpected moan from me as my lips fell slack. He grinned against my mouth in satisfaction and swirled his tongue inside. God, the man could kiss. It nearly made me weak in the knees.

My arms wrapped around his neck as my fingers threaded through his hair and pulled him impossibly closer. There was a raw hunger in him I had never seen before.

He ran his hands up my thigh and under the short dress I wore. Most of my pants were getting tight in the waist so dresses had become my go-to clothing for the first time in my entire life. As his hand continued its upward trek, and he made fast to dispose of the simple cotton underwear I wore beneath, I thought maybe dresses in general needed to be reconsidered. I could get use to such easy access.

Bran's hand was everywhere and persistent. I was already panting with need when he lifted me with his other arm and carried me the few steps to the kitchen table. He set me on top as he reached for his buckle.

There was no further build as he lifted my dress and thrust himself into me in one fluid motion. I leaned back against the table and groaned as he grabbed my hips and set a hard and steady pace that had me withering in moments. Even through my first orgasm he continued his penetrations. He faltered his pace only slightly on my second. My vision was darkening at the edges and my body spent in sheer ecstasy by the time he finally came hard within me, so hard that it triggered a third that left me quaking in my own skin and unable to speak as I lay on the table.

Bran collapsed on top of me. He kissed my stomach before rising and lovingly cleaning me up.

I finally sat up, still shaking from the greatest sex of my life. He wrapped his arms around my waist and helped steady me before kissing me again. My head was spinning, dizzy with love.

"You're forgiven," I finally managed to say softly.

It caused a deep laugh to rumble through him. He looked at me with so much love in his eyes that my heart nearly burst with happiness. He brushed a stray hair that was plastered to my cheek with sweat.

"Is that all it takes?" he teased.

"My sisters are always going on about how incredible makeup sex is. If that's what they've been talking about, then mister, you and I are going to fight a lot from now on."

The buzzer on the stove went off, bringing me quickly down from cloud nine. I started to jump down off the table and stir the soup I had on, but Bran told me to stay put and took care of it himself. I sighed watching him. Was there anything sexier than a man cooking?

Flashes of him standing over me just a few minutes earlier brought a smile to my face. Okay, was there anything sexier than my mate?

He dished big bowls of soup for the both of us and brought them to the table. I slid off the table to sit in a chair next to him.

The mood between us quickly turned from giddy to solemn.

"We need to talk," he finally said.

I knew whatever he had to say wasn't good. It was likely the reason we came home so quickly. I could feel the sense of doom upon us and wasn't sure I wanted to hear it.

"Look, I don't want you hearing about all this after-the-fact, and there are things you need to know about me. Physically you're prepared and I know you will protect our child against anything life throws your way. But there are things about me that you don't know, Ruby. Things I don't want you to know, but that you're going to hear about anyway."

"Bran, you're freaking me out," I said. "What's going on?"

"You don't need to be scared. It's going to be okay. You're both going to be okay," he assured me, but the fact that he wasn't including himself in that statement terrified me.

"You're leaving us, aren't you?" I accused, trying to stay calm. Everything was going perfectly. Why would he just leave us?

"Yes, but not in the way you think, sweetheart."

"Don't you dare call me sweetheart during this conversation."

"Ruby, calm down. It's not what you think. Will you please just let me explain?"

"Fine," I said, holding back all my redheaded temper. "Explain." I crossed my legs, then crossed my arms over my chest, and waited.

"*Po dyavolite!* This is harder than I thought." He scrubbed his face with his hands and took a deep breath. "Thomas and I leave for Westin Pack in an hour. I don't have much time left."

"What? We just got home from there. Why are you going back?"

"Because I have to finish what I started, and that is only going to end in one way. I'm so sorry. I don't want to leave you. I don't want to leave our baby, but it's the only way. I didn't come here looking for work like I told you. That was a lie. The last thing I ever expected was to find you. To fall in love with you."

He looked so defeated it was breaking my heart, but I had to hear it all. I had to know the truth.

"Go on," I said with a stronger voice than I felt.

"My name is Branimir. I shortened it to Bran to sound more American. I'm not from the former Indiana Pack. To the best of my knowledge, no one survived from there. It made it an easy, indisputable pack. My father was Kamen, Alpha of the Bulgarians. My brother Nicholai now carries that title."

I tried not to react, but a gasp of shock escaped.

He either didn't notice or didn't care as he continued. "I had sworn my allegiance to another and accepted a position to come here as a spy seeking revenge for my father when my brother refused to make threat against the Westins. You have to understand, Ruby, I was so filled with hate and anger. There was so much darkness in me. You changed that. If I could go back and do it again, would I change a thing? I don't know. I hate that I am bound to this plight, held accountable by an unbreakable blood oath that only ends in one of two ways—Kelsey dies, or I die. Either way, we both know my life is about to end. She is weak, and even with this distance the oath calls to me. It burns through my blood with indescribable pain. But despite it all, even knowing what's about to come, I'd do it all again, because otherwise I never would have met you. You wouldn't be expecting my child. Even in death I will be forever grateful for the time we had together. It was the happiest of my entire life. My only regret is that I can't stay. I have no right to ask anything of you. I know I don't, but as selfish as it is, I want our baby to know how much I loved him, or her, and how much I adored you. Never doubt that, Ruby."

I watched as his hand reached out to me, then pulled back. I took it and placed it against my cheek.

"You aren't getting away from me that easily, Bran. You're my mate, for better or for worse I will stand by your side."

I felt a strange shift in my stomach. At first I thought it was gas, but it happened again. My eyes spilled the tears they were holding back.

I took his hand and moved it from my cheek to my stomach and watched in awe the moment he felt our child move for the first time, too.

"I think someone's saying we're all in agreement about this."

Bran

Chapter 25

Bringing Ruby along was not part of the plan, but despite Thomas's objections too, neither of us could tell her no. I would much rather her last memories of me be of our time making love in bed up until the moment came to leave, but in the end it had been her decision and final wish.

I was resolved to my death and what I had to do, but that didn't curb the pain from the oath. If anything it was worsening the closer we got. I struggled to hold the dagger in my hand as it throbbed.

"It's getting worse?" Thomas asked as we landed and found a car waiting to take us to Kyle's.

"Yes. I think it must be sensing the end is near and is spurring me on to the finish," I admitted through gritted teeth.

As we arrived back at the house, the burning sensation was almost unbearable.

"How did you know?" Liam asked the second we walked into the room. Patrick tried to silence him, but to no avail. "What the hell, Bran? How did you know Conlin was a spy?"

"Conlin?" Thomas asked.

"I guess I forgot to fill you in on that with everything happening today," I said as an apology to Thomas.

"Conlin was the one responsible for Kelsey's accident. He cut the brake and power steering lines. She didn't stand a chance on the road," Patrick said, filling him in. "All evidence pointed to Wyatt."

"Wyatt?" Thomas said angrily. "No way in hell would Wyatt do something like that."

I cringed at the accusation. No one could say for certain how anyone would react given the situation. He hadn't believed me capable of poisoning my own mate either, yet I had.

"Bran told us it wasn't Wyatt and had us recheck Conlin for connections with the Bulgarians," Liam said. "So again, how did you know?"

"Fecking hell. Liam, Bran's a Bulgarian spy, too," Patrick finally admitted.

Kyle shook his head. He'd been standing off the side, quiet since I'd walked in. "I trusted your brother with this peace treaty," he admitted, looking distraught.

"You were right to," Thomas told him. "Continue your peace treaty talks with Nicholai. He is not our enemy. Appears there's another who has stepped up and is preying on those that feel revenge for Kamen's death is still justified. They aren't pleased with the peace treaty making for easy targets," Thomas told him.

"Who?" asked Patrick. "I need a name."

"I cannot give it to you," I told him, sadly. "His identity was sealed by an Alpha gag order. You will not break Conlin for that answer either, though I know he and I serve the same Alpha," I told him. "He warned me there were others. I do not know how many or who. I had only just put together the possibility of Conlin being one of his spies when I told you to look deeper into his past."

Ruby stepped up next to me and took my hand for support. I hated that she was there, but I took the love she offered freely anyway.

"I don't understand how you could do this to your mate," Kyle accused.

"You worry about your own mate, Kyle," Ruby warned him.

"Ruby, that's enough," Thomas scolded.

"I know Thomas already filled you in on everything, Kyle. Where's Kelsey? I'd like to just get this over with," I said.

It felt so wrong. Like I was saying, "Hey man, where's your mate so I can go ahead and kill her, then you can kill me and everything will be fine, except I guess you can't really kill me, cause you'll be dead, but no worries, 'cause I'm gonna let her kill me anyway." That was basically what this had come down to and we all knew it, except apparently for Liam, because he was looking more confused the longer this took.

"Where's Conlin?" Thomas asked, entirely changing the subject.

"He's being held in the kitchen, actually. Do you want to see him for yourself before they take him to lockdown?" Patrick asked.

"Bring him in," he said.

Two large men I didn't know dragged a beat-up looking Conlin into the room and set him down before Thomas.

"You are not my Alpha. I have nothing to answer to you for," he said. He turned to look at me in disgust. "Coward," he spat. "I practically handed her to you on a silver platter and you still didn't have the balls to finish the job. I doubt you ever will, but then again, I don't think you'll be around much longer from the looks of things, but our Alpha will certainly have a fine time with your pretty mate there after you're gone."

I shook in rage as fur sprouted across my hands and up my arms. Ruby held on tightly and begged me to calm down.

"Don't let him get the better of you. Not the likes of him," she said calmly until my breathing began to stabilize and the fur rescinded.

"I'm only the first of many coming to right the wrong you made in harboring the Alpha she-witch. Branimir is a testament to the truth I speak. He may not have the stomach to end her life, but can he resist the call of the oath that pumps through his blood? I'm afraid I'll never know, but rest assured if he doesn't, others will follow. It will never end until the witch is dead." He gave a half-crazed laugh that made Ruby shiver next to me.

The door at the end of the hallway opened and Kelsey came into view.

Conlin smiled at her with a far-off look in his eyes. "Oh look, speak of the devil. Your time has come, beloved one. Dagger at the ready."

I turned to look at Kelsey for the first time as Ruby screamed. I looked back to see Conlin foaming at the mouth and violently convulsing. I grabbed my mate and buried her face in my chest.

"What the feck?" Patrick said as he jumped up and ran to Conlin's dead body.

"Cyanide," I said calmly. "He broke his tooth. Like some old World War II practice, we're all outfitted with it. I've never actually known anyone to use it before, though."

"You have that inside you, too?" Kyle asked in shock.

I nodded.

"Why the hell didn't you just use that then?" he asked.

I laughed. "You serious? Did you see that? I'm not dying that way."

Ruby smacked me. "This isn't a time to be joking about things like that."

I looked up and my eyes met Kelsey's. "Hello, Elena," I said respectfully. To her left stood an old face I hadn't seen in several years. "Raina. You're alive."

"Hello, Branimir," she said.

Rumors had come back to us that Raina had disappeared, never to be heard from again. Yet here she stood, alive and well. I knew she was Kelsey's aunt, so I shouldn't have been too surprised.

"Hi, Bran," Kelsey said. "I truly wish we were meeting under better circumstances."

"As do I," I told her honestly.

"Ruby, what are you doing here? Please don't make this any harder than it has to be," Kelsey said. "I do not enjoy killing for any reason, but especially a needless one. Isn't there anything we can do?"

Ruby took a deep breath and turned to her. "We've gone over every possible scenario. There's no way to break the oath without one or both of you dying."

"A challenge situation seems like the most humane way to handle things. Kyle discussed it with you already, yes?" Thomas asked.

Kelsey nodded and sighed. "I thought all this was behind us."

"He will never stop," I warned her. I passed Patrick a USB thumb drive loaded with as much information and files as I could muster while working around the gag order. "That's as much information as I can offer. I truly hope it helps you take him down once and for all."

"You could have killed me sooner, Bran, and you didn't. We can work something out," Kelsey offered.

I shook my head, resolved in my fate. "I'm afraid not. I've already tried and in doing so I hurt the only two people in this world that matter to me. I can't risk their lives. The oath is growing stronger. The pull of it is too much. The pain is unbearable. The only relief I get is in the active pursuit of your demise, or in death itself. I know how my story ends, Kelsey. I'm sorry to put this burden on you, but you have a family of your own and those boys need their parents. You have to fight me. You have to kill me," I told her.

Thomas and Kyle looked on helplessly. No one wanted it to come down to this but there was no other way. I desperately needed the pain to go away. Patrick tossed her a sword. I turned one last time to kiss my mate a final goodbye, and pulled out my dagger.

The searing pain that shot through my hand made me cry out as I dropped the dagger and fell to my knees.

"What the hell?" I yelled. "I'm doing everything he asked. The pain should be lifting, not worsening."

"Maybe your heart's not into it?" Liam offered.

"I've given up everything. I'm resolved to my own death," I said.

"That's it," Patrick offered. "Maybe Liam's right and you don't really have any plans to kill Kelsey, just to let her kill you, so it's not enough. I think you have to pick up the dagger with the intentions of actually killing her."

I looked at the two of them as if they were insane. "What do you think I'm touching the dagger for at all? I know I have to actively move to attack her. I'm telling you, I can't."

I reached for it one last time, and screamed out at the fire it caused. My blood felt as though it were boiling.

"Kyle, I'm not doing this," Kelsey said stubbornly. "Look at him. This isn't self-protection, this is blatant murder. I won't have any part in it."

"Kelsey, you have to," I practically begged her.

Raina calmly walked over and picked up the dagger. She turned it over in her hands, studying it.

"Branimir, stand up," she finally said. "Tell me what has changed."

"Nothing. Nothing has changed. The oath was very specific," I tried to explain.

"They usually are," she said sadly. "What were the exact words of the oath?"

I thought back, remembering the moment vividly. "'I swear to enact the wishes of my Alpha or die trying.'"

She considered each of my words as the rest of the room waited silently, watching to see what happened next.

"And how did the witch that forged the oath reply?"

"She said, 'It is done. From this moment forward you are bound by blood to obey the wishes of your Alpha.'"

"Your Alpha," she considered. "Is it possible his wishes have changed?"

"Never," I admitted.

"Wait a sec," Thomas interrupted. "Pick up the dagger again."

I looked at him like he was insane, but I obeyed. This time there was no pain whatsoever.

"What the hell?" I asked, not for the first time.

"Raina, is it possible that the oath he took is truly bound to him and him alone?"

"What do you mean, Thomas?" Kyle asked.

"Like she said, if the witch specifically said the oath was tied to the wishes of his Alpha, then if his Alpha's wishes changed, he'd know it from the dagger's spell, right?"

"Yes, but you heard him, there's no way that would happen," Kyle reminded him.

Dawning finally set in and I stood a little taller. "But what happens if my Alpha changes?"

"Exactly," Thomas asked.

"You mean, you give your allegiance freely to another Alpha?" Raina asked. Thomas and I nodded. "If you're remembering the phrasing correctly then in theory the oath would transfer to the wishes of your new Alpha, but surely someone as powerful and paranoid to put you in this situation and issue a gag order against his identity wouldn't be arrogant enough to overlook a simple binding spell to keep your allegiance."

Thomas and I looked at each other and broke out into huge smiles. He embraced me and I could feel his relief. When he stepped back, I grabbed Ruby by the waist and pulled her against me, then I kissed her with a fresh new outlook on life.

"Everything's going to be just fine," I assured her.

Kelsey was next, as I let go of Ruby and pulled her into a hug. Kyle, Patrick, and Liam all growled behind me, but Thomas covered my back to intervene and held his hands up to stop them.

"I swear I'm not going to kill you," I finally told her.

"Good, because there's no way I was going to be able to kill you either," she confessed.

A loud ear-piercing whistle rang out and I turned to see Patrick with two fingers still in his mouth.

"What the bloody hell just happened?"

Kyle moved to physically take his mate from my arms, and Ruby quickly found her way back to them.

"The Alpha called Bran yesterday while he was here and threatened Ruby. I guess more of a promise to take them and 'care' for them, than a threat, but Bran ran home as fast as he could begging me to take him into the Pack so that I could protect her and their child upon his death."

"But you knew he was a traitor and you accepted him into your Pack anyway?" Liam asked, still looking confused.

Patrick smiled and slapped him on the back. "Bloody damn good thing, too, I'd say."

"I had to protect my family, no matter what," I said, more to Ruby than anyone else in the room.

"How do you feel?" Ruby asked, starting to worry over me.

I took a quick examination. All the pain was gone. The burning in my veins was gone. I felt better than I had in months. "I'm good. Really good," I said.

She kissed me and her smile lit up the room.

"And to be clear, you no longer wish to kill my mate?" Kyle asked.

I shook my head. "Truth be told, I never wanted to kill your mate, but more importantly, my Alpha doesn't want that, either."

I elbowed Thomas in the ribcage and a festive feeling filled the room.

Ruby

Epilogue

In the days and weeks following the day Kelsey and Bran tried to face off, life for us changed quickly. He didn't get off scot-free. There were consequences to being a traitor, but where most men in his position would have been put to death anyway, Kyle and Kelsey gave him clemency.

In fact, Kyle surprised us all by issuing a gag order of his own that nothing said that day left that room or was discussed outside of the people present. And, even further shocking, Thomas sealed the order. A double Alpha gag order was unheard of and not something that could ever be tampered with.

Patrick had suggested with the new power Thomas held over my mate that he should consider using it to his advantage. To work off penalties they'd agreed upon, Bran was now training under Patrick's guidance as Collier Pack's new head of security. There were a few restrictions in place, too, but the majority of them meant my mate was home each night with me. He wasn't allowed to travel without Thomas or Patrick at his side, which was also fine by me. Everyone knew I was a homebody anyways. It also meant that Bran would never be considered a traitor outside that room. They had done it for me and for the child that continued to grow in my womb.

Now in my third trimester, that child still needed a name. He or she was a stubborn one, for sure. It had taken three ultrasounds before Doc had successfully determined our child's sex. We had joked that at this point we might as well be surprised, but my sisters rallied together, determined to throw us a big gender reveal party.

Lily and Doc were the only two people who knew what we were having.

Everyone was in town for the party and I nervously lay in bed the night before still debating over names. Since Bran and I couldn't seem to agree on anything, we had decided that if it was a girl, he would get to name her, and if it was a boy, I could choose. The problem was, I had no idea and no name to give if it turned out we were having a boy.

"Go to sleep. We have a big day tomorrow, mama," Bran said.

"I can't sleep."

"Excited?"

"Nervous!"

"What? Why would you be nervous?" he asked.

"I haven't named our child yet," I confessed.

"Really? You were adamant you wanted the boy's name."

"I know, but I'm worried you'll think it's stupid, and I can't come up with anything else."

Truth was, I'd been wracking my brain for weeks and only one boy's name ever stuck out to me.

"It's going to be a girl anyway, so don't worry about it," he said, like there was no doubt in his mind.

"Why do you insist it's a girl?" I asked for the millionth time.

"I don't know. Wishful thinking, I guess."

"You want a daughter?"

"I can't imagine anything greater than a little mini-you."

"You're just trying to be sweet. I bet you don't even have a name picked yet, either."

"Actually, I do."

"Do not," I insisted.

"Yes I do, and no you aren't going to coax me into telling you before the reveal tomorrow. These were your rules, remember?"

"Oh God, it's Jordan isn't it?"

"Jordan is a great little cowgirl name, but no, you made it painfully clear how much you hate that name. I just hope you don't hate this one."

"Better tell me just in case," I tried, but he wasn't budging.

He wrapped his arms around me and kissed the top of my head. "Go to sleep, Ruby."

I tossed and turned until dawn, frustrated that Bran had no trouble sleeping whatsoever. When the sun started peeking out, I slid out of bed and took a quick shower. I was used to restless nights as my protruding belly was making it harder to get comfortable more and more each day. I knew it wasn't because of that, though. This time was just sheer nerves.

After my shower I dressed and grabbed a granola bar. Bran was still fast asleep. I walked down to the dairy and found Clay already hard at work. I swore he was an even bigger workaholic than I had ever been. I was proud of him, though, as he was thriving in his new position, and I was surprised to find I didn't feel put out by the work he was doing. There really was room for the both of us and we were making it work.

"Hey Ruby Red," he hollered out, and waved when he saw me. "So today's the big day, right?"

I nodded. "Yup. I'm kind of nervous. Lily wouldn't tell me anything about the party."

"My understanding is she kept it to family only, and the Six Pack, because we are family."

I nudged him with my shoulder. "You are family," I confirmed.

I walked around doing my rounds. Nothing was out of place. Everything was under control and I knew Bran would still be sleeping when I walked upstairs. Except, to my surprise, he was up. He had two cups of tea on the table and waiting for my return.

"You're awake?" I asked and he rolled his eyes as I feigned shock.

"Smart-ass. Come have a cup of tea," he said, carrying the cups to the coffee table. I sat down on the couch feeling like the size of a house. I seemed to always be hot and uncomfortable these days and I still had eight weeks left to go.

Bran's hand rubbed over my stomach. "You know, it sort of feels like it's always been the three of us, but somehow finding out what you are in there just seems to make it all the more real," he said, talking to my belly. He did that a lot these days.

"You're a goof," I said. "It's still just the two of us for a couple more months."

He sighed and sat up to kiss me. "I'll take it."

I looked around the apartment. It was a mess from all the construction. Bran and Thomas had gotten a little out of control. When they were done, the apartment would be six times its original size and take up much of the top level of the dairy barn. In addition to the nursery, there were two more bedrooms, two full baths, and an office for Bran. I wasn't convinced they'd be done before this little one arrived, but they all promised me it would.

We sat and talked and just enjoyed each other's company. I had told him that he was being ridiculous, but I knew what he meant about everything feeling more real today. The baby had been just an abstract idea and today it would be a he, or a she.

"It's about time to head over," he finally said.

"Do we have to?" I asked.

He laughed. "I'm pretty sure we do."

"Fine." I pretended to pout, but rose and walked into the bedroom to put on the dress Elise had picked out for me.

Everything that had happened had bought us closer to Patrick and Elise. Just another bond between the Collier and Westin Packs. E had become yet another sister to me and she had fabulous taste in fashion.

I twirled around, admiring the dress and feeling pretty despite being the size of a whale.

Bran let out a low whistle. "Wow, you look amazing!"

I blushed. "Thank you." I turned to look at him and helped him adjust his tie. "You clean up pretty good yourself there, 'daddy.'"

We rode over to the Alpha house together. Everyone was there when we arrived, and the place had been transformed into a pink and blue wonderland. As I'd figured, Lily had gone all out. Mom got to me first and hugged me closely.

"I still can't believe my baby girl is having a baby," she gushed.

Austin ran around taking bets on the gender.

We ate lunch first and by the time the spotlight was truly placed on us, I was an even bigger ball of nerves.

Lily took center stage. "Welcome everyone, and thanks so much for coming out to celebrate the upcoming arrival of a new Collier pup. I couldn't be happier for Ruby and Bran. They've overcome far more in their time together than most couples will face in a lifetime and I have no doubt it has helped prepare them to be the best possible parents for my new little nephew . . . or niece," she said after a slight hesitation. "So let's get on with it and see what we're having. But first, the proud mother and father have had a bit of a struggle. Turns out while they agree on most everything in life, coming up with names was not one of them." Everyone laughed. "So, Ruby, if you're expecting a little boy to the family, what will he be called?"

All eyes were on me as I gulped. It was my moment of truth. I looked at Bran and knew I'd chosen right. "Branson," I said. "Son of Bran."

Bran smile and everyone clapped and cheered. He nodded his approval as someone yelled out, "That's a fine little cowboy name!" That caused quite a few chuckles.

"And Bran, if we're expecting pink, what's her name to be?" Lily asked.

Bran winked at me. "We're going to stick with my precious gemstones. Her name will be Opal."

"Opal?" I asked, and I immediately loved it. He hugged me and gave me a quick kiss as I wiped back tears. "I love it."

"Okay, well, the moment of truth is here," Lily said, trying to sound dramatic. Oscar carried out a large black balloon and held it up in front of us. "Pop the balloon to reveal the gender."

She handed us each a really long pin or crochet needle of some sort. I wasn't even certain what it was. They counted down and Bran and I each stabbed the balloon with it. Nothing. Our friends and family started to laugh.

Bran held the balloon in his arms, and I stabbed it harder. Nothing. We couldn't pop the balloon. Oscar volunteered to sit on it, and he bounced around a few times before we gave up on that. Everyone was shouting suggestions and Lily was apologizing.

"I swear, it was supposed to pop. This shouldn't be happening," she said.

At last Bran reached into his boot and pulled out his dagger. It was no longer a threat to us, but it still made me nervous anytime I saw it. He winked and stabbed the balloon with a loud pop.

Pink confetti went flying everywhere as cheers and tears went up all around. Bran had a huge perma-grin on his face as he twirled me around. Once I was back on my feet, he kneeled before me and kissed my stomach.

"Hi there, Opal. Mommy and I can't wait to meet you."

Dear Reader,

Whew! This one was a big of a whirlwind, but I hope it was worth it all. If you enjoyed this book, please take a second and drop me a review.

Next up for Collier Pack will be Peyton's story. I think her mate Oliver will really make you swoon! It's on schedule to release in May 2019. I'm also working on Midnight Promise, book 3 in my ARC Shifters, and finishing up writing Under a Harvest moon, the Mary and Jason Westin prequel featured in the Fated Mates boxset coming June 4, 2019. Lots of awesomeness in the works!

For further information on my books, events, and life in general, I can be found online here:

Website: www.julietrettel.com

Facebook: http://www.facebook.com/authorjulietrettel

Facebook Fan Group: https://www.facebook.com/groups/compounderspod7/

Instagram: http://www.instagram.com/julie.trettel

Twitter: http://www.twitter.com/julietrettel

Goodreads: http://www.goodreads.com/author/show/14703924.Julie_Trettel

BookBub: https://www.bookbub.com/authors/julie-trettel

Amazon: http://www.amazon.com/Julie_Trettel/e/B018HS9GXS

Much love and thanks,
Julie Trettel

SNEAK PEEK

FATED MATES

Featuring

Under a Harvest Moon

A Westin Pack Prequel

By

Julie Trettel

Coming June 4th, 2019

Mary
Prologue

I looked across the table, my heart filled with joy and overflowing in love. Each of my children continued to humor me with my mandatory Tuesday night dinners, or at least all that were able to. I missed my Lily but was so proud of everything she and her mate, Thomas were doing in Collier Pack. I was proud of every one of my children, their mates, and the grandchildren they continued to bless me and my ever-growing family with.

My eyes connected with my handsome mate and I smiled. Nearly thirty years had passed, and he still made my heart flutter every time he looked my way.

"Mom, are you sure you don't mind babysitting again this weekend?" Liam asked.

"You did just have the boys last week. We don't want to be a burden," his mate, Madelyn added.

"Mom, if it's too much, just say no. It's okay. We know little Jason is a handful and still not overly fond of the bottle," Kyle said.

"Would you all just stop. I love having my grandsons stay the night, and Jason and I did just fine last week. We'll be fine again," I tried to assure them. "I did raise five near perfect kids with minimal permanent damage, you know."

"Well, there is Lily," Chase said jokingly causing his siblings to chuckle.

I gave him a stern look and enjoyed watching him squirm in his seat. No matter how old my children got, I could still get them to behave with one simple look.

"You guys go, enjoy yourselves. It's one night. The babies will be fine. Oscar and Zander will help me with them. Right boys?"

"Yes ma'am," Oscar piped up.

Oscar was my son Liam's boy. Actually, he was Maddie's son, conceived from a horrifying rape. That girl had been through so much. A lesser man may have walked away from the two of them even as true mates, but not my Liam. He had taken the steps to officially adopt Oscar and was fiercely protective of the child. I couldn't be prouder. Oscar would always hold a special place in my heart. He was a good boy, and he took after his daddy in more ways than one, starting with his fierce protectiveness of his baby sister, Sara.

Sara was Liam's biological daughter, but in our eyes, there was no distinction. In my house, you were either family or you weren't. Period.

My oldest son, Kyle and his mate Kelsey had blessed us with my other two grandsons, Zander and little Jason, named after his grandpa, my mate.

Chase and Jenna were still young and in college, so I'd give them a pass on growing our family further. . . for now. But I didn't understand what the holdup was with Elise and Patrick. They had been mated almost as long as Kyle and Kelsey and I was beginning to fear they couldn't conceive.

While I had been immensely blessed with children, it was a known fact that many of our kind struggled in that department. I had begged her to speak with Micah, our local Pack doctor, but she had only laughed and said it would happen in time and she wasn't ready for kids yet anyway. That had led me to believe maybe she was doing something to prevent getting pregnant, but it broke my heart to even think that.

After dinner, the kids helped clear the table, but I shooed them out of my kitchen and out of my house when they tried to help with dishes.

"Go," I insisted.

"Your mother's right. You're intruding on our grandparent time now," Jason said.

I wrapped my arm around his waist and squeezed as we watched them all leave. Both babies were content in the playpen I kept permanently set up in the living room and Oscar had already put a movie on for him and Zander.

Jason and I sat on the couch just enjoying watching them. He leaned over and kissed the top of my head. It was a simple night. The best kind of all. Not for one second of a day since the awful attack had I taken him or my family for granted. The little tedious things had become a joy as I knew each and every day was a gift, a blessing from God.

When Kyle had mated Kelsey, we didn't know much about her or her background. The secrets that had unraveled around that girl had led to war with the Bulgarian Pack. Jason had been Alpha at the time and did not hesitate to protect our Pack and our family, including Kelsey, but it had nearly cost him his life. Since we are fully and wonderfully bonded, I almost followed him into death. It was one of the most surreal moments of my life, but Kelsey had saved us.

Alpha powers had transferred to Kyle at that time and Jason and I had made the decision not to fight that. They began giving us grandchildren quickly which helped soften the blow and keep us from boredom. Chasing after four little ones kept us young while reminding us constantly that we were anything but.

When the movie was over, it was time to put the kids to bed. Oscar would be allowed to come downstairs and read or often play a round of chess with his grandpa, but the little ones needed to stay to their routine.

I went into the kitchen to fix two bedtime bottles then Jason and I each snatched up a baby from the playpen and headed upstairs to the nursery.

I sat in one rocking chair while he sat in another as we fed and lulled Sara and Jason to sleep.

"Tell us a story, Grandma," Oscar begged.

"Yeah, the good one about you and Grandpa," Zander added.

"That's my favorite, too," Oscar said.

"You mean the one where your grandmother tried to run me over with a car?" Jason asked.

The boys laughed.

"That never happened," Oscar said.

He sounded so certain that I couldn't break his perception of a mating between us. Of course I knew exactly what story they wanted to hear. They asked me to tell it every time they came over. The boys loved hearing sweet stories of me and my mate, and this one was their favorite, and it had been a favorite amongst my children as well. I smiled as I launched into the tale.

The first time I met Jason I was six years old. Of course, I knew of the Alpha's son, but he was almost five years older than me and I had only ever seen him from a distance before then. He was taller than the other boys his age, and when one of them came and picked on my friends and I, Jason defended us. He had been like a knight in shining armor.

I went home that night and I told my mama, "When I grow up, I'm going to marry that boy."

"What boy?" she'd asked.

"Jason Westin," I'd said proudly with all the hope and love of a young girl's crush.

My mama laughed. "Little one, shifters don't marry, and Jason Westin is going to be Alpha someday. He'll mate someone very special who will be our next Pack Mother." Then she proceeded to explain the difference between mating and marrying telling me that love played no part in it and grumbling that Grandpa shouldn't let me watch so much television, that it was corrupting me to human ways.

"But you were that someone very special, right Grandma?" Oscar interrupted as little Zander nodded his head and smiled.

I let my mind wander back to the days of my youth all leading up to one very special night. Things hadn't been quite as simple and perfect as the stories they heard from us led them to believe.

Check out more great books by Julie Trettel!

The Compounders Series

The Compounders: Book1
http://www.amazon.com/dp/B018HKIU7O/?tag=kp-jtret-20

DISSENSION
http://www.amazon.com/dp/B01N6FSGLE/?tag=kp-jtret-20

DISCONTENT
http://www.amazon.com/dp/B07215QYL1/?tag=kp-jtret-20

SEDITION
http://www.amazon.com/dp/1624870678/?tag=kp-trettel-20

Westin Pack

One True Mate
https://www.amazon.com/dp/B071HXL3R2

Fighting Destiny
https://www.amazon.com/dp/B07575HC9T

Forever Mine
https://www.amazon.com/dp/B077V9WHMG

Confusing Hearts
https://www.amazon.com/dp/B07BP9XL9W

Can't Be Love
https://www.amazon.com/dp/B07DCCRB58

Collier Pack

Breathe Again
https://www.amazon.com/dp/B07F6KN6G3/

Run Free
https://www.amazon.com/dp/B07KFNY1DH/

ARC Shifters

Pack's Promise
https://www.amazon.com/dp/B07J5455XG

Winter's Promise
https://www.amazon.com/dp/B07MBXM36R

Midnight Promise
Coming Soon - April 2019

Fated Mates Box Set

Fated Mates
https://books2read.com/FatedMatesCollection
Coming June 4th – pre-order today!

About the Author

Julie Trettel is author of the Compounders and Westin Pack Series, a full time Systems Administrator, wife, and mother of 4 awesome kids. She resides in Richmond, VA and can often be found writing on the sidelines of a football field or swimming pool. She comes from a long line of story tellers. Writing has always been a stress reliever and escape for her to manage the crazy demands of juggling time and schedules between work and an active family of six. In her "free time," she enjoys traveling, reading, outdoor activities, and spending time with family and friends.

Visit

www.JulieTrettel.com

Made in the USA
Las Vegas, NV
23 January 2022

42148521R00108